BODIE: THE DAY OF THE SAVAGE

The day a Kiowa Indian saved Bodie's life was one that neither of them would forget. In Long Walker, Bodie found the nearest thing to a partner he'd ever need. They were both hunters, outcasts, loners — and they were both on the trail of a bible-spouting killer called Parson Kane. However, they discovered that even as a team they may have bitten off more than they could chew . . .

Books by Neil Hunter
in the Linford Western Library:

NEIL HUNTER

BODIE: THE DAY OF THE SAVAGE

Complete and Unabridged

LINFORD
Leicester

First published in Great Britain

First Linford Edition
published September 1994

British Library CIP Data

Hunter, Neil
    Bodie the stalker no.6: the day of the savage.
    —Large print ed.—Linford western library
    I. Title II. Series
    823.914 [F]

    ISBN 0-7089-7591-7

Published by
F. A. Thorpe (Publishing) Ltd.
Anstey, Leicestershire

Set by Words & Graphics Ltd.
Anstey, Leicestershire
Printed and bound in Great Britain by
T. J. Press (Padstow) Ltd., Padstow, Cornwall

This book is printed on acid-free paper

This one is for my parents . . .
with a special thank you

1

HECTOR DIAZ came out first. The battered swing doors of the saloon were smashed aside as he burst through. He was hatless, his thick black hair tangled and greasy. His clothes were soiled and wrinkled, and he was sporting a heavy growth of stubble on his broad jaw.

"Come on then, Bodie, you *gringo* son of a bitch! Here I am! You been waitin' for somebody to come out — so here I am!"

Diaz rattled the long-barrelled Winchester he was holding, his dark eyes raking the dusty, deserted street of Dry Fork. Silence greeted his challenge. Diaz swore loudly.

He stepped to the edge of the boardwalk, dusty boots clumping on the worn boards, his heavy Mexican spurs dragging across the wood.

"Bodie! You come out, an' let's get this over! I wan' kill you! When you dead, Bodie, I'm goin' to cut off your *cojones* an' feed them to the do . . . !"

There was a movement across the street. A mere flicker, and then a rifle barrel winked in the sunlight a fraction of a second before a shot rang out — followed by two more in rapid succession.

The bullets hit Diaz in the chest. With undiminished force they ripped through Hector Diaz's body and out between his shoulders. Blood spewed from the wounds, spattering the board-walk and the saloon frontage. Diaz, already dying, was driven backwards. He smashed bodily against the front wall of the saloon, twisting in a muscular spasm, and fell face first through one of the big, decorated windows. Glass shattered and filled the air around Diaz's plunging body. It seemed to hang above him in a glittering cloud — then struck Diaz as

2

it followed him to the floor.

The echoing gunshots were ringing across the rooftops as Bodie stepped into view, cutting across the street in the direction of the saloon. Hector Diaz had not been alone in the saloon; he'd had two companions with him when he had turned up in Dry Fork — and they were still somewhere inside the saloon. Bodie wanted to get to them before they organised themselves in the first minute or so following Hector Diaz's death.

He reached the boardwalk and crossed it in a couple of long strides. Holding his rifle across his chest Bodie went in through the swing doors, hitting the saloon floor on his left shoulder. He rolled, twisting his long body across the scuffed boards.

There was a movement on his right. A gun blasted, loud in the confines of the low-ceilinged room. The bullet whacked a pale splinter of wood out of the floor. Sharp chips stung Bodie's face. He kept moving, jerking the rifle

3

round, finger easing back on the trigger as he caught sight of a dark figure stepping out of the gloom on the far side of the saloon. The Winchester jolted in Bodie's hands as it fired. The bullet splintered one of the stair bannister supports. Boots thumped on the floor as the hunched figure of a man sprang away from the shadows around the staircase.

Bodie held himself still long enough to trigger a further shot. It caught the running man in mid-stride, throwing him sideways against the bar. He hung there for a moment, struggling to stay on his feet while blood streamed from the wound in his chest.

Knowing that there was a third man somewhere in the saloon Bodie kept moving, working his way towards the staircase. He heard the soft thud of the man he'd shot slumping to the floor.

Another sound followed on. It came from a higher level, above Bodie's head. The manhunter tried to pinpoint it but could only place it somewhere on the railed balcony running around the upper gallery. Bodie swore softly. Whoever it was up there he had a damn good edge on anyone down on the saloon floor.

Bodie realised fast that he was in the worst place he could be. He got his feet under him and thrust himself upright, heading for cover. There was a scuffle of sound from overhead. A rifle blasted. The bullet whacked a white hole in the floorboards. It was close — too damn close, Bodie thought, and reckoned that the rifleman would have him pinpointed by now. He lunged forward, knowing he'd cut it fine, maybe too fine. He was angry with himself for not allowing time to make a shot himself.

He heard a shot, tensing automatically. No bullet touched him, nor did one strike the floorboards. Bodie heard a man grunt, a hoarse, pained sound. He twisted, throwing a frantic glance towards the balcony — and saw a blurred figure topple forward over the railing to smash face down on the saloon floor.

Bodie turned around and faced the saloon door. Framed in the door was a tall, broad-shouldered figure. Bodie couldn't see the man's features too well because the sun was streaming in through the open doorway, leaving the figure in shadow. But he did see the smoking rifle held in the big hands.

"You want me to say thanks? Or give you a share of the bounty?" the manhunter asked.

"Don't want either, Mr Bodie!" The voice was deep, with a slightly husky quality to it.

"Well, hell, I'll buy you a drink then!" Bodie snapped.

The shadowy figure gave a chuckle. "You do that and we'll both be back in trouble!"

Bodie reached the doorway and the tall figure stepped aside to let him pass. On the boardwalk Bodie glanced over his shoulder, and a wry smile began to etch itself around the corners of

6

his taut mouth as he stared at his rescuer.

He found himself eye to eye with the tallest, meanest-looking, full-blooded Kiowa Indian he'd ever come across.

2

"**M**Y father called me Long
Walker," the Indian said,
falling in alongside Bodie as
they crossed the street. "On account of
my legs," he added. "But you can call
me Lon."

Bodie glanced at his unwelcome
companion, trying to figure out why
a Kiowa Indian, dressed like a goddam
cowhand, should turn up out of the
blue to save his life; because that
was what had happened, and like it
or not — which he didn't — Bodie
was obligated to Lon Walker.

"I been trailin' those three for close
on a week," Lon said casually. "Cut
your tracks two days ago and followed
you in."

Son of a bitch, Bodie thought. Let
me do all the dirty work and then steps
in like some guardian angel wearing

feathers! Which wasn't true in fact — but the image was as close as Bodie needed to get.

"What you on?" he asked. "A scalphunt?"

Lon laughed dryly. "Hell, no, Bodie. What do you think I am — some kind of savage?"

They reached the adobe building hung with a weatherbeaten sign that read: Marshal's Office. That was all it was: just a single room with a desk at one end and a low cot at the other. Dry Fork, being less of an actual town and more of an extended way station trying to improve its image, didn't even run to a cellblock in its jail — not that there had ever been anyone requiring incarceration.

"You comin' in with me?" Bodie asked. "Or you got some medicine to make?"

"You keep talking like that, Bodie, and I'm going to start wonderin' if I did the wise thing taking that Comanchero off your back!"

Bodie cuffed his hat back, sleeving sweat off his face. "And there I was thinking you were all heart."

Dry Fork's part-time lawman, an overweight, one-eyed man named Carson, was spread out in a large cane-bottomed chair just inside the door. He'd been sitting there for most of the morning, all through the seige over at the saloon, and in that time he hadn't moved once; except to lift a bottle to his thick lips every now and then.

"They're all yours, friend," Bodie said from the door.

Carson swivelled his one good eye up to settle on the manhunter. He belched noisily. "What the hell am I supposed to do with 'em?" he wheezed.

"Mister, you can do whatever takes your fancy," Bodie snapped. "All I want is your name on a piece of paper to say I delivered 'em!"

Carson sniffed, a sly grin edging his soft mouth. "What do I get out of it?" he asked.

Bodie didn't say a word, but suddenly he was standing over Carson, his big hands taking hold of the fat man's grubby shirt. He yanked Carson up out of the seat and propelled him round the desk and slammed him down in the hard chair. The bottle Carson had been holding flew from his fingers and smashed against the wall. Thin fingers of cheap whisky trailed down the flaking adobe.

"You got the paper?" Bodie asked.

Carson nodded. He was almost crying. He fumbled in a drawer for the appropriate document.

"Pen?"

"Yeah! Yeah, I got one!"

"Get it done, friend," Bodie suggested.

The only sound for the next few minutes was the laborious scratch of Carson's pen on the paper. When he had eventually completed the task Bodie picked up the paper and read it through. He grunted his approval, folded the document and tucked it in his shirt pocket.

"Thanks for your hospitality, Marshal," he said. "And for your invaluable help during the action!"

Bodie turned on his heel and strode out of the office. It was only as he stepped outside that he remembered Lon Walker. The tall Indian was leaning against the wall of the jail.

"You still here?" Bodie asked. "Ain't there a cigar store in town you can stand outside?"

Lon grinned. "If you're figurin' on insulting me so I'll go away, Bodie, you better keep trying, 'cause it's been tried by experts."

Bodie shook his head. "Ain't nothing left for me to do so I'll just have to take you with me while I eat."

"Hell, whiteman, now you talk language I savvy!"

Bodie led the way to the far end of the street. A dingy adobe building stood a little way back from the rest. A long time back somebody had painted a sign onto the adobe. The weather had faded it and the flying dust had sanded

12

much of the lettering away; there was enough remaining to identify the place as a cantina. A rattling bead curtain hung in the doorway. Bodie stepped through, Lon close behind him, and they walked into a long, shady, cool room with a low ceiling. There was a bar at one end of the room. The rest of the space was taken up by a scattering of tables and chairs. Bodie chose one in a corner of the room where he would be able to look out through the window.

"You wish a drink, senors? Maybe food?" The question came from a thin-faced Mexican who held his skinny hands at his waist, rubbing them together unceasingly. His voice had a whining tone to it that irritated Bodie.

"Food," Bodie said. "What've you got?"

"There is some very fine lamb stew," the Mexican said.

"Bring it for two," Bodie said. "And coffee."

The Mexican bobbed his head and scuttled off behind the bar where he disappeared through a door.

"All right, Lon Walker," Bodie said. "You know why I'm after Preacher Kane and his bunch. What's your story?"

"Three weeks back Preacher Kane's Comanchero's raided my people's village. They burned it to the ground. Killed all the old folk and the babies and took the healthy men, women and children captive. Some of the young men were out hunting. When they found what had happened they went after Kane's bunch. They were ambushed and slaughtered. By the time I heard about it there wasn't a thing I could do except try and free the ones Kane took captive."

"Where were you?"

Lon's brown face hardened. "While my people died I was living in the whiteman's world, as I have done for the past three years. I turned my back on my people because I saw the

14

way ahead. The Indian doesn't have a future if he carries on in the old way. He has to change. To throw away the old customs and learn to live as the white does. It's what I did, Bodie. I took a job herding cows. I learned to wear boots and a hat. To sit a saddle. I learned to smoke and play cards and a few other things. And I earned money. I took a lot of hard knocks at first, but when I proved I could do the job as well as any man the other drovers quit pokin' fun at me."

"But?"

"I'm still a Kiowa. The blood is still Kiowa, and when Kane and his butchers made my people bleed he made me bleed too."

"So you figure to bury the whole bunch?"

"I didn't know the whiteman had cornered the market in vengeance," Lon said evenly.

Bodie studied the Kiowa as they ate their meal. Lon Walker was one hell of a mystery. It was almost like talking with two separate people. One minute he was a Kiowa, eulogising about his tribal responsibilities — the next he was talking like any forty-a-month-and-found cowboy straight out the Big Bend country.

Over a cup of poor coffee Bodie said, "I ain't a man for partnering, Lon. Been too long on my own. Got my own ways of dealing with a situation and it don't make any consideration in respect of anybody else. When things happen they tend to happen damn fast. No time to talk over with a partner what the best way is of handling it." He glanced at Lon, slightly annoyed because the Indian didn't appear to be paying all that much attention to him.

"Sure, I know what you mean, Bodie," Lon spoke up. He raised his eyes and stared at Bodie. "I'm the same myself. But there are times when a man can't allow himself the luxury of choosing his own way."

"Yeah!" Bodie growled. "So it looks like we're stuck with each other. I figure it'll make things a sight easier if we both know what the other's up to."

"Don't seem likely either of us is going to step down an' leave the field clear."

Bodie only smiled at that. It was a smile devoid of humour, cold, almost cruel. The smile of a wolf already hot on the trail, with the scent filling his nostrils, single-mindedly tracking down his quarry — and there was no way to divert him from that course.

3

"**K**ANE is no true Comanchero," Lon remarked as he and Bodie loaded the supplies they had purchased onto their respective horses. "He would steal from the Comanche themselves if there was something to be gained. He is nothing but a renegade. A crazy man who enjoys the spilling of blood."

Bodie swung into the saddle, checking his restless horse. With Lon riding close on his left side he turned his horse north and then slightly west, leaving Dry Fork to its aimless existence. Ahead of them lay endless miles of empty land, a sunbleached, dusty wilderness that reached as far as the meandering Rio Bravo, and then on into Mexico. It was rumoured that Preacher Kane had some protected haven in the wilds of Chihuahua — a place where he could rest, where his Mexican contacts brought him customers for the white and Indian women he took over the border. There was a town close to the border, so Bodie had been informed, that served as a kind of gateway into Mexico. The information had reached Bodie via Lannigan, the manhunter's boss during the days when Bodie had worn a US Marshal's badge. Lannigan had lost two of his men who had been working under cover, trying to get some evidence of corruption against the law in Petrie; the fact that he knew something was going on but helpless to stop it angered Lannigan; the deaths of his two men angered him more; so he took the strictly unofficial step of passing on his information to Bodie, knowing full well that the bounty hunter would use it in his strictly unsubtle, though effective, way.

It took Bodie and Lon four long, hot, dusty days to reach Petrie. It was a hybrid community — a curious

Mexican-American blending of buildings and people. It was also one of the most inhospitable places Bodie had ever come across. Even Lon commented on this fact as they rode along the town's main street.

"You get the feeling we ain't exactly welcome?" he asked.

Bodie grinned tightly. "I've seen friendlier faces at a hanging."

"How do you want to go about getting what we come for?"

They reined in at a sagging hitch post near a small eating house. Bodie climbed stiffly out of his saddle, looping his reins over the weathered rail.

"I've got a feeling it'll come to us," he said.

They strolled casually up onto the boardwalk, moving in the general direction of the eating house. Bodie slapped dust from his pants. Outside the eating house he paused, taking a thin cigar from his shirt pocket and lighting it with exaggerated slowness while he took a long look over the town. He heard the measured tread of heavy boots moving in his direction, only turning when they were almost on him.

The three burly figures spread across the boardwalk had badges pinned to their dirty, stale-smelling shirts. Bodie eyed them indifferently; if they were lawmen, he decided, then he was a horse's ass!

"You want to come by?" he asked, stepping to the edge of the boardwalk.

His remark caught them off balance, blunting any edge they might have had. One of them made an abrupt gesture with his hand.

"What you doin' in Petrie?" he demanded.

"Brother and me figure to have a meal," Bodie said.

The one who had spoken threw a quick glance at Lon, his face colouring angrily. "You tryin' to be funny mister?" He jabbed a thick, dirty finger at Lon. "He's an Indian!"

Bodie shook his head, glancing at Lon. "See, I told you he'd spot the difference."

"Look, mister, you cut the crap! Last thing this town needs is a funny man! Now you talk straight. What're you doin' in Petrie?"

"Minding my own business, friend," Bodie snapped, all the humour removed from his tone. "And until you can tell me what law I've broken — keep out of my way!"

The deputy who had been doing the talking let his right hand slip towards the butt of the gun holstered on his hip. As he did Lon drove the barrel of his rifle across the man's knuckles. The deputy gasped, snatching his hand away from his gun.

"Goddam!" he said.

"That was a damn silly thing to do," Bodie said to the deputy. "I should have told you my friend here gets a little jumpy when people make sudden moves. So when you boys walk away, do it nice and slow."

The other deputies glanced at Lon, who had his rifle pointed in their direction. Any thought they might have been harbouring drifted away. They backed along the boardwalk for a few yards then turned and slouched off in a tight group, as if they were all feeling the pain of the injured man and suffering with him.

"The way the law works in this town," Bodie said, "I reckon we've just committed a hanging offence."

He led the way inside the eating house. As they entered, a sharp-faced little man stepped hurriedly back from the curtained window.

"We're closed!" he scowled. He wore glasses. Behind the lens his eyes were red-rimmed and watery.

Bodie glanced round the small room. Most of the tables were occupied.

"No, you're not," he said. He and Lon sat down at an empty table.

"I can't . . . " the little man began. Then he broke off. "I don't want any trouble!"

"Long as you don't burn my food you won't get any," Bodie said.

"I don't have to serve you," persisted the little man, his voice rising sharply. "I can say yes or no!"

"Say yes," Bodie suggested. "Be easier on everybody."

The little man threw a pleading look in the direction of his other customers — but they had all become extremely interested in their meals.

"You eat then get out," the little man said to Bodie and Lon. "I don't need your trouble." He turned and headed for the steaming kitchen at the back of the building.

"One hell of a nervous town," Lon said.

"Maybe they got reason to be nervous," Bodie said. "Couple of dead lawmen ain't exactly the easiest kind of skeletons to have in your closet."

"You figure they're jumpy enough to hassle every stranger who rides in?"

"Could be."

The meal came a little while later. Bodie ate slowly, conscious of the tension in the air.

The door opened with a crash and the three deputies eased into the room. A fourth man followed them. He was tall, with unusually broad shoulders. His brown face was severe, his mouth little more than a bloodless slit. He was dressed all in black and high on his left hip he wore a long-barrelled Colt, butt forward and angled across his belly. He paused just inside the door, hostile eyes raking the assembled customers.

"Everybody out!" he rapped. "Now!"

Chairs scraped against the floor. A knife clattered against a glass. Half-eaten meals were forgotten as there was a general exodus towards the door.

"You reckon he wants us to leave as well?" Lon asked hopefully.

"Uh-uh. Something tells me we're the main attraction."

The black-clad man crossed over to their table. The silver badge pinned to his shirt glittered each time it caught the light. He positioned himself in front of the table.

"One of the rules I like to stick to," said the man in black, "is the right to question anybody I figure needs questioning!"

"Mine is not answering questions while I'm eating," Bodie said.

"The hell you say! Mister, you know who you're talkin' to?"

This time Bodie actually raised his eyes from his plate. He glanced up at the man. "Sure," he said. "You're the feller who's spoiling my lunch!"

"You're making it easy for me to get angry, mister!"

"Look," Bodie said, "it doesn't make any difference to me if you want to carry on playin' the fool. You go ahead — but I'm finishing my meal."

"Son of a bitch!" the man yelled. "We'll see who's the foo . . . !"

He had grabbed for his gun as he spoke, swinging the long barrel in Bodie's direction — but the manhunter had moved before the weapon cleared the holster. He rolled sideways out of his seat, swinging his right foot up into the man's groin. It struck with a soft thud, drawing a howl of agony from the pursed lips. He stumbled back, his gun swinging towards the ceiling.

There was a moment when the room stilled — and then it literally exploded with violent action.

Bodie lunged up off the floor, head down, and hurled himself at the three deputies as they came towards him. The force of his forward motion drove them back across the floor. One of them collided with a table and went down with a heavy crash. Curling his fingers over the butt of his gun Bodie slid it from the holster, swinging it up and round, the hard length of the barrel clipping one deputy under the jaw; the man gave a strangled yell, clutching his hands to the gash that was spurting bright blood. Out of the corner of his eye Bodie spotted the remaining deputy dragging his own handgun into play. Jerking his body to one side Bodie felt heat from the muzzle-flash as the gun went off, the bullet chewing a ragged hole in the floorboards. Closing his hand over the barrel of the gun, Bodie forced it aside and slammed his shoulder against the deputy's broad chest. He rammed the man against the wall and heard him grunt softly. The deputy's face twisted into an angry mask, lips peeling back to expose his stained teeth. He lifted a hard knee, aiming for Bodie's groin. The blow never landed. Bodie's Colt smashed down across the deputy's skull, opening a raw gash that spilled blood down the man's face in glistening streaks. A second blow drove the deputy to his knees, pitching him face down on the floor.

Bodie turned away from the falling deputy. He was halfway round when a gun went off. Something caught him a stunning blow on the side of his head. The room blazed with brilliant light, which faded just as swiftly, plunging Bodie into total darkness. Dimly he heard more shots, each one growing fainter and fainter, and then there was nothing . . .

4

SOMEBODY woke him by tossing a bucket of cold water over him. Bodie swallowed a mouthful and half choked. He rolled on his side, and noticed that he was lying on a stone floor. He lay for a while, coughing up more water, wishing that the fierce throbbing inside his skull would go away.

Without warning a boot smashed into his left side. Pain burned its way to his very gut. He heard movement close by. Then strong hands caught hold of his wet shirt and he was dragged to his feet. Before he could get his balance he was thrust forward. At the last moment he saw the stone wall rushing at him; he was too late to avoid it. The impact made him gasp. He felt blood ooze from the cut on his left cheek. Somehow he stayed on his feet, turning away from the wall, facing his attackers.

They were all there. The three deputies and the big man dressed in black. None of them appeared to be in a friendly mood.

"All right, you son of a bitch!" the black-clad man said. "You want to explain this?" He thrust out his hand. There was a sheet of paper in it. Bodie only needed a quick glance to recognise it as the claimer for his bounty money, signed by the one-eyed marshal back in Dry Fork.

"What's to explain?" Bodie asked. "It's legal."

"Legal? Haw!" one of the deputy's snorted. "Tell that to Preacher!"

"Shut your mouth, Mose!"

"Now you got problems," Bodie said.

"*I* got problems?"

Bodie wiped a smear of blood from his mouth. "I just said that."

"I've heard you've got some kind of a hard reputation, Bodie. Let me tell you, mister, it don't scare me. I ain't no half-growed kid out lookin' to make his name. I made mine a piece ago. Likely you heard of me — Buck Dade."

The name stirred a distant memory in Bodie's mind. The face had started him thinking, though the action had been subconscious; too much had been going on at the time. Now it came to him. Buck Dade had been something of a minor gunfighter seven, maybe eight years back. He'd been involved in a number of incidents, hiring out his gun during a spate of short-lived range wars in Texas and New Mexico. Then about three years ago he'd dropped out of sight. At the time Bodie had wondered what had become of him; now he knew.

"They do say if you wait long enough a rat eventually crawls out from the hole it's dug," said the manhunter.

"From what I hear, Bodie," Dade sneered, "you ain't exactly gone up in the world. From US Marshal to bounty hunter"!

"It's a living."

"Could be the death of you, Bodie."

"Hey, Buck," grumbled the deputy named Mose.

Dade glanced at him, frowning, as Mose leaned in close and spoke. Dade shook his head, Mose mumbled fiercely.

"All right! Take Cushman with you," Dade said. "If you find him — bury him there! I don't want him brought back! Understand?"

"Yeah! Sure, Buck!" Mose said. "Hey, Cush, you come with me!"

The two deputies crossed the room, leaving by a heavy wooden door.

"You won't catch him," Bodie said, making a calculated guess they'd been talking about Lon Walker; it was Bodie's first thought of the Kiowa; obviously he had got clear during the fracas in the eating house — which was fine for the Indian.

"I think we will," Dade grinned. "Mose and Cushman are damned good trackers. Better than a lot of Indians I know!"

"Thing is," Bodie said, "you've got to get him one way or another!"

Dade's expression hardened. "Meaning what, Bodie?"

"Hell, Dade, we all know what you're up to here in Petrie. Playing watchdog for Preacher Kane and his bunch!" Bodie knew he was pushing his luck. If Dade decided that he'd been exposed he could easily kill Bodie on the spot. "Way I see it, your time's just about up!"

"The hell with you, Bodie!" Dade yelled. "I figure you're bluffin'. I don't reckon you know as much as you want me to believe."

"Why don't we kill him, Buck?" asked the remaining deputy.

"Because dead he can't tell us a damn thing, Tully. I don't aim to cut and run until I know the game's been bust wide open."

Tully moved across the room in Bodie's direction. He slid a thick, leather-bound club from his rear pocket, swinging it in his big hand.

"You want him to talk? He'll talk!"

Buck Dade caught Bodie's eye. "Believe him, Bodie. He could get a month-old corpse talking."

Bodie put his back to the wall, tension washing over him. His aches and pains were blanketed as his body readied itself for the action ahead.

"You going to tell Dade what he wants to hear — or do I beat the shit out of you?" Tully asked; he was starting to smile, his face glistening with oily sweat.

"Go f––– yourself!" Bodie said.

Tully stiffened as he absorbed the suggestion. In anger he lashed out with the club, a mistimed blow aimed at Bodie's skull.

It was easier than Bodie had anticipated. Tully's blow missed by inches. As the deputy's body followed through, his bulk turning in towards Bodie, the gun holstered on his hip jutted in Bodie's direction. It took no longer than a second for Bodie to snatch the gun from its holster. As it slid into his hand Bodie leaned in towards Tully, thrusting the gun at Buck Dade, hammer back and triggering . . .

His first shot caught Dade high in the left shoulder, blasting away a pulpy chunk of flesh. Dade was spun round in a circle. This meant that Bodie's second bullet ripped through Dade's back, tearing into the chest cavity and out the front in a gush of blood and tatters of flesh. Dade threw his arms wide as he pitched face down on the slab floor.

Tully, regaining his balance, made a grab for the gun. He failed to reach it, and moments later he felt the muzzle of the gun jam into the flesh of his side. His ears rang to the blast of a shot. There wasn't even time to scream, to register a protest at the way his life was being abruptly and brutally ended. Tully's eyes glazed with shock, mouth falling open in an empty gesture. His body shuddered under the impact of the .45-calibre bullet. It cleaved through flesh and living organs, pulverising anything in its destructive path. Tully was hurled aside, blood spouting from the gory hole made by the bullet's exit from his right side. He hit the floor hard, squirming in agony against the pain flooding his body, blood spattering the stone slabs around him.

Bodie swung the smoking Colt towards Buck Dade. The man was still alive; in pain and coughing up blood, he had dragged himself against the wall. Sweat beaded his face as he tried to lift and cock his own heavy gun. Bodie crossed the room in quick strides, kicking the weapon from Dade's trembling hands. The man's ashen face, creased with pain, jerked upwards, angry, defiant eyes staring at the manhunter.

"I should have remembered you were a tricky bastard!" he said.

"Beats the hell out of being smart," Bodie observed. He crouched beside Dade. "Now — you want to tell me all about Parson Kane?"

"Go to hell," Dade scowled.

"You got a doctor in this town?" Bodie asked.

Dade frowned. "Why?"

"I could get him to come and look at you."

"You son of a bitch!" Dade hissed. "By God, you'd do it too! Let me die while you sat and watched! You miserable bas . . . !"

Bodie rapped him across the mouth with the barrel of the gun. Something snapped in Dade's lower jaw. He groaned, his head flopping back, blood dribbling from one corner of his slack lips. After a minute he shook his head slightly, raising it a little. Slowly he opened his eyes and saw that Bodie had replaced the gun with a knife he'd plucked from one of Tully's boot-tops.

"What're you aiming to do with that?" Dade asked. He spoke slowly and with difficulty, his face already badly swollen where Bodie had struck him.

"Trying to make up my mind where to start cutting," Bodie said. "I figure I owe you, Dade. Hospitality ain't one of your strong points. Since I've been in Petrie you sons of bitches have parted my hair with a bullet, kicked the hell out of me, and done everything possible to get me upset. And you've done that all right — so now it's my turn, Dade, and the more I think about it the more I'm starting to like the idea!"

Dade tried to bluff it out. "You trying to scare me, Bodie?"

"No. Just tell you I ain't playing games . . . and Mr Dade, you'd better believe it!"

A nervous twitch started in the corner of Dade's bloody mouth. He tried to force a confident grin. He still didn't believe Bodie would use the knife. He carried on thinking that way up to the moment Bodie made the first cut. That was when he started screaming . . .

5

PETRIE had the appearance of a ghost town.

Bodie emerged from the jail, pausing to buckle his retrieved gunbelt. He checked the Colt, then eyed the deserted street. He didn't trust what he saw. Somewhere out there were Dade's remaining deputies, Mose and Cushman. Bodie wondered whether they'd located Lon. Or had he found them? The Kiowa was no novice. Bodie grudgingly admitted that the Kiowa carried a great deal of sense inside his head — it hadn't been Lon who'd ended up in the cellar of Petrie's jail! Cut it out, Bodie cautioned himself.

He stepped casually down to street level, boots crunching the gritty earth. He could sense the eyes watching from behind shaded windows along the street. They were all there — the

40

good citizens of Petrie — waiting for somebody to get shot. Bodie wondered who they'd prefer dead — him or Dade's gunslingers?

Towards the north end of the street a figure stepped into view from between two buildings. There was something familiar about the man. Bodie watched the figure move up the street, boots dragging in the dust. It was the deputy called Mose.

The heavy Colt in Bodie's hand began to rise. The approaching Mose didn't seem to be aware of him. A frown creased Bodie's face as he walked out to intercept the deputy.

The deputy stumbled, halted, eyes rolling skywards. He took another step, faltered, then fell face down in the dirt. Bodie was close enough to see the heavy-bladed knife sunk deeply between Mose's shoulders. Blood had spread in a wet, dark patch down the back of his shirt.

Lon! It had to have been Lon!

Bodie twisted round, scanning the

41

length of the street. Nothing. Damn! Where was Cushman! Maybe Lon had already taken him . . .

He almost missed Cushman. The deputy burst into sight fifty yards along the street, ran a few feet then dragged himself to a halt as he spotted Bodie. He lifted the rifle he was carrying and loosed off a jerky shot. It whacked up a spout of earth a yard short of Bodie. The manhunter cut off across the street, then angled towards Cushman. The deputy levered another round into the breech of the rifle, swinging the muzzle round in an attempt to keep it on Bodie. Even while he was doing that Bodie changed direction again, lunging forward and throwing himself flat. Cushman's eyes flickered wildly, head jerking. The rifle barrel traversed, the muzzle dropping. Bodie steadied his Colt with his left hand, let his finger caress the light trigger and felt the gun lift as it fired. Cushman's head rocked back, a dark hole appearing just above his right eye. The back of his skull exploded outwards and Cushman went over backwards, hitting the dusty earth with a heavy sound. Blood began to pool under his shattered skull, soaking rapidly into the dust, and a booted foot kicked, heel gouging the earth . . .

Bodie climbed to his feet, slapping dust from his clothing, and cursing softly in the aftermath of violence. His stomach held a greasy sickness and there was a nagging pain from a knock he'd given himself when he'd dropped to the ground.

He stood alone in the middle of Petrie, lost for the moment, drained as the adrenalin filtered away and the excitement faded. He let the moments slip by, watching and waiting to see if there was any more trouble coming his way.

"Hey, Bodie!"

He turned at the sound of his name and saw Lon Walker walking along the street. The Kiowa looked totally relaxed, almost indifferent to the taint of violence in the still air.

"Looks like I could have saved myself the trouble," Lon observed. "I was working round to pulling you out of that place." He ran his eyes over Bodie, noting the blood and the bruises. "They give you a hard time?"

"They figured to. So I had to change their minds some."

"You pick up anything on Kane and his bunch?"

Bodie nodded. "Dade — that was the feller in black — he told me everything I wanted to know."

"Wouldn't have pegged him for the helpful sort," Lon said.

Bodie smiled. "He discovered he liked talking to me!"

Lon moved by him and vanished into the jail. He came out again after a couple of minutes to find Bodie still waiting for him in the middle of the street. The Kiowa crossed to where Mose lay and pulled his knife from the corpse. He glanced over his shoulder at Bodie.

"You sure you ain't got any Indian

blood in you, Bodie?" he asked, still seeing the scene that had confronted him in that room below the jail.

"Can't say for sure. Only thing I remember is my grandma always got a gleam in her eye if anybody mentioned Chief Joseph."

Lon smiled briefly, a low, almost inaudible chuckle rising in his throat.

Cautious figures began to emerge from the stores along the street. Slowly at first, then with quickening paces, they converged on the two dead deputies. Guarded glances were cast in Bodie's direction, eyes averted swiftly when they found the manhunter returning their gaze.

"You want to get out of here?" Bodie asked, and caught Lon's nod.

They trailed down the street and picked up their waiting horses. Mounting they turned and rode out of Petrie, Bodie leading the way.

Before dark they crossed the shallow flow of the Bravo and rode across the dusty bank on the Mexican side. They were in Chihuahua now. If they had been working outside the law on the American side, here they were beyond its help. There was little love lost between the law enforcement agencies of the respective countries. Too much political manoeuvring had soured what link there might have been. Now each country eyed the other, always distrustful, always wary. Any American who ventured into Mexico went with the knowledge that he was on his own. He took his chance and paid the price if he gambled and lost.

They made camp in a lonely canyon that sheltered them from the chill winds of the dark night. The winds blew in from the north, slanting down off the high peaks, swiftly erasing the lingering heat of the day. Bodie built a small fire beneath a wide overhang to keep the reflection hidden. He cooked a quick meal and boiled up a pot of coffee, then damped down the flames and stood the bubbling pot in the hot embers. Lon joined him and they ate in silence, each lost in his private thoughts. After the meal Bodie went and stood watch while Lon took a few hours rest. Later they changed places. Bodie wrapped himself in his blankets and slept.

He was roused, seemingly only minutes later, by Lon. Shrugging off the blankets Bodie snatched up his rifle and followed the silent Kiowa to a ridge overlooking the wide expanse of land they still had to cross. It was already light, though the warmth from the newly risen sun still had to drive away the bitter remnants of the long, cold night.

"There," Lon said. "To the east. About a mile off."

Bodie blinked away the haze of sleep, following Lon's finger.

"You see 'em?" asked Lon.

"Yeah! I see 'em."

"Yaquis!" Lon said softly, with respect edging his tone.

"Damn!" Bodie said forcefully. He'd heard enough about the Yaquis to realise that they could be in for a

47

hard time. The Yaquis, the Indians of Mexico, were said to be blood-kin to the Apache. It was also said that they were far fiercer and more savage than their Apache cousins. Bodie wasn't too worried over that, though he wasn't going to bother if he didn't make contact with the Indians.

"I think we'd better get out of here," Lon said. "If we have to face 'em I'd rather do it in the open."

They slipped quietly back to where they'd left the horses, saddled up, and broke camp. Walking the horses they left the canyon behind. As soon as they reached open ground they climbed into the saddle and rode on. Despite the threat of the Yaquis they rode slowly, letting the horses set the pace. It was cool now, but the sun would soon flood the land. There was little to be gained by tiring the horses.

The morning drifted by. Bodie and Lon picked their route carefully, making certain they left very little in the way of tracks. They didn't fool themselves into thinking they would lose the Yaquis so easily. All they could hope to do was delay the Indians.

Towards noon they angled their horses down a long slope dotted with tangled brush and tall cactus. Pale dust drifted in the still air at their passing. At the bottom of the slope a shallow creek reflected the bright gleam of the sun, and the horses lifted their weary heads as they caught the scent of water.

Lon slid his rifle into his hands as they neared the creek. He worked the lever gently, saying nothing as Bodie glanced at him; the manhunter was aware of the implications of Lon's actions. The horses stopped at the water's edge, dipping their heads to drink. It was very quiet. Heat danced across the surface of the water.

Without moving his head Lon said: "We're not alone."

Bodie dismounted, closing his hand over the stock of his Winchester and sliding it from the sheath. He was between the horses, his actions concealed from watching eyes. He levered a round into the rifle's breech.

"They're in the brush over to the left," Bodie said. "Twenty, maybe twenty-five feet."

"I know," Lon whispered. "That's too damn close even for me!"

Even as he spoke there was a burst of movement and three brown figures erupted from the brush. They were short and stocky, faces broad, black hair streaming behind them as they leapt across the sunbaked earth.

Bodie stepped out from between the horses, his rifle up and firing at the bobbing, weaving Yaqui. Close by, Lon's rifle added its sound to the din. One of the Yaquis twisted sideways, arms and legs flailing wildly, blood spurting from ragged wounds.

An answering shot whacked a long furrow in the hard earth just ahead of Bodie. He sighted the Winchester on a lunging figure, triggering shot after shot, powder-smoke lashing back into his face.

A second Yaquis stumbled, a shrill scream tearing from his throat. The naked brown chest dissolved into a pulsing, bloody mess of torn flesh and splintered bone. He smashed face down onto the ground, his wiry body heaving in a final spasm of agony.

The third Yaquis vanished from sight. One moment he was there, the next he was gone. Bodie ran forward, searching the area before him. He knew his prey was out there somewhere, belly down on the ground, merging into the surrounding terrain.

Bodie indicated to Lon that they should get down themselves. He knew that while the Yaqui could probably see them, they couldn't see the Indian.

After a few minutes Lon asked. "You hot, Bodie?"

"Damn right," Bodie muttered. He could feel oily fingers of sweat working down his back. "Way things are, even if that Yaqui doesn't get us, we'll probably burn to a crisp."

A little while later Lon asked, "Bodie,

how good are you with that rifle."

"Good enough. Why?"

Lon laughed softly. "Because I'm going to give you a chance to prove it. And, Bodie, you'd better be ready!"

Before Bodie could raise an objection Lon stood up, glancing around him with the air of a man who felt fairly safe. He began to walk forward, searching the terrain, giving a pretty good imitation of casual relaxation. He was putting on a good show for the waiting Yaqui, Bodie decided. He couldn't fault the Kiowa on courage, though he might question Lon's good sense. He was taking one hell of a chance, and his only reward might be a bullet in the gut.

Nothing happened for what seemed an eternity, though Bodie realised no more than half a minute had gone by. His eyes ached from scanning the rocky ground ahead of Lon, searching for any telltale movement. Any sign that might show where the Yaqui was hidden. He wondered if the Indian had figured out what they were up to and was refusing to take the bait. It was one possibility. There was also the chance that the Yaqui had gone, slipping away while Bodie and Lon had been working out what to do; it was possible but, Bodie decided, unlikely.

It happened fast. One minute there was only Lon's tall figure . . . and then there was a lithe, brown shape rising up from the earth. But not in front of him. The Yaqui came up behind Lon, and even Bodie hadn't suspected the Indian was so close.

The Yaqui's abrupt appearance almost caught Bodie napping. He saw the Indian, caught a glimpse of the short-barrelled rifle lining up on Lon's broad back, and yelled a warning to the Kiowa. In the same moment Bodie jerked his Winchester round and pulled back on the trigger. Lon began to turn. The Yaqui hesitated at Bodie's shout, his head snapping round, his lips drawn back in a savage snarl.

In that brief fragment of time Bodie's Winchester exploded. The Yaqui stumbled, half turning towards Bodie as his right side spouted blood and flesh. For a moment it looked like he might go down, but somehow the Yaqui stayed on his feet, his own rifle pumping shot after shot in Bodie's direction. He was firing wild, but Bodie wasn't. He put two more bullets into the Indian, the savage force lifting the Yaqui, screaming, off his feet. His chest fountained red, pulped flesh exposed. He hit the ground on his back, kicked briefly, and then became still.

Lon walked by the dead Yaqui, watching Bodie climb to his feet.

"At least you weren't lying about being good with the gun," he said.

Bodie turned and walked to his horse. He swung into the saddle and rode off. Lon caught up with him, shoving his rifle back into its sheath.

"We make a good pair, Bodie," he said.

Bodie glanced at him. "You mean we kill people good?" His voice was flat, empty. He jerked hard on his reins

54

and rode on ahead.

For a moment Lon studied him, a puzzled look on his brown face. He clicked his teeth. "Damn me, horse," he said, "if I live to be a hundred years old I still ain't going to figure these white sons of bitches." Then he shrugged his wide shoulders. What the hell use was there worrying over the matter? He had enough on his mind already.

6

SQUATTING behind a slab of bleached stone they watched the activity in the village below them. It had taken them three days to reach the place, riding across a silent and empty land, with only the sun and the sky for company. In all that time they hadn't seen another living soul. It was as if the land around was barren, a vast tract of sand and stone and brush. It was a harsh, ungiving land, burned dry by the pulsing heat thrown down out of an endless curve of blue sky. They had ridden in silence, minds dulled by the stifling heat, bodies aching, the sweat sucked from them. The pale dust soured their throats and stung their eyes. Conversation had lapsed, and when they did speak it had been in short, snapped monosyllables. Finally reaching the village had been on a par with discovering an oasis in the desert. They were simply content at first to sit and observe.

"Bodie, you sure this is the place Dade told you about?" Lon asked.

The manhunter glanced across at the Kiowa, his eyes narrow against the glare of the sun. "I'm sure," he growled. He was itchy and dirty and not in the mood for too much talk.

"I hope he was telling you the truth."

"We'll find out," Bodie said, and suddenly tired of just sitting he got up and went to his horse. Mounting up he reined his horse about and turned it downslope, in the direction of the village.

As Bodie reached the rutted trail leading to the village Lon reined in alongside him. They were greeted on the outskirts of the village by a half-starved mangy dog, the size of a wolf. It bared its jagged yellow teeth as it stood in their path, deep snarls rolling up from its throat, causing their horses to pull back.

"You want to talk to it in Spanish?" Bodie asked dryly.

Lon muttered something and dismounted. He walked towards the dog, ignoring its hostile growling. When he was no more than a couple of feet away he lunged forward and grabbed hold of the animal at the back of its neck. Lifting the surprised beast into the air he swung it without effort, completing a half-circle before he let go. The dog's snarling turned into a long howl of anguish as it struck the ground in a dusty tangle. It skidded on its haunches for a few yards before regaining control of its limbs. When it did it threw a terrified glance in Lon's direction before it scuttled out of sight between two adobe huts.

"I hope the two-legged ones are as easy to handle," Lon said.

He took his horse and led it into the village, Bodie riding beside him. Bodie let his eyes range back and forth across the seemingly deserted area covered by the village. He knew that they were being watched. From behind every door, at every window, the dark, expressionless eyes would be watching.

They reached the centre of the village. In the middle of the dusty plaza was a well with a stone-built church, its walls bleached by the pitiless sun. A tall, single bell tower seemed to cant back against the pale sky.

"Nice to feel welcome," Bodie said softly.

Lon spat in the dust, blinking his eyes against the glare of the sun bouncing back off the white adobe buildings. "I want a drink," he said and tramped across the plaza to the well.

Bodie leaned forward, crossing his arms over the saddlehorn, and listened to the silence around him. He could feel the hot sun on his back. It was making him drowsy. He heard the creak of the rope lowering the bucket into the well, and suddenly he felt very thirsty.

"Hey, Bodie, you want some water?"

Lon's voice was loud, booming across the empty plaza. He hauled the dripping bucket into sight and placed it on the stone wall.

Bodie climbed off his horse and joined him. They fished their tin mugs from their saddlebags and dipped them in the bucket. The water was clear and cold, tasting fresher than anything they had tasted for a long time.

"Bodie, this is one hell of a quiet place," Lon remarked. "Like being in Petrie all over. Hell, just look around. What do you see?"

"Damn all," Bodie agreed. "There were plenty of folk around when we were up on that hill."

"And when they saw us they hid. That's normal for a Mexican village — but I would have expected someone to have shown by now."

"Something's keeping them away," Bodie said. He glanced at the Kiowa. "Do we smell *that* bad?"

Lon laughed. "Likely we do. More likely they're scared of something."

"Maybe they figure we're some of Kane's bunch."

"Could be," Lon said. He turned to the bucket and started to splash water on his face.

Impatience turned Bodie away from the well. He snatched his hat from his head, slapping dust from it. He'd only taken a couple of steps away from the well, his eyes wandering with little interest over the front of the church, when he spotted three riders coming in at the far end of the village.

"Lon!"

The Kiowa glanced up, brushing his wet hair away from his face. "I see 'em!"

"They strike you as the welcoming committee?"

"Hell no!"

The riders walked their horses across the plaza, drawing rein a few yards short of the well. Two of the riders were Americans. The third was a lean, hard-eyed Mexican dressed in black, his pants and short jacket trimmed

61

with silver. Even the wide-brimmed sombrero he wore was black. His lavish costume was completed by an ornate gunbelt, richly decorated and supporting a holstered, silver-plated handgun.

"What do you want here?" The Mexican spoke with the tone of one well used to commanding respect and instant obedience.

He received neither of these things. An uneasy silence followed his question. A nerve flickered below the Mexican's left eye, a sign that he was angry. He turned his attention to the tall, hard-looking American.

"You! What is your name? Why are you on the land of Don Castillo?"

"Castillo?" Bodie held the Mexican's stare. "Hell, I never heard of him!"

"Nor me," Lon said. "He some kind of bandit or something?"

"Looks like we found us a couple of comedians, Rivera," one of the Americans said. He was stocky, wide-shouldered, dressed like his partner in faded, dusty clothing. One cheek of his unshaven face bulged outwards from the thick wedge of tobacco lodged there, and his crooked teeth were stained from the juice.

"They will not find it funny when they stand before Don Castillo," the Mexican answered. He flicked his hand at the waiting horses. "You two will mount up and come with us! Pronto!"

Bodie casually put his hat back on. He raised his eyes to the Mexican's face. "Go to hell, you son of a *puta*. We ain't going anywhere with you. Now just ride out, or you're going to find out what it's like having your *cojones* torn off and stuffed down your throat!"

The stocky American made a choking sound in his mouth. His face darkened in anger and without warning he drove his horse forward, directing it at Bodie. As the animal lunged forward Bodie stepped aside, and he saw that the American's right hand had dropped to his holster, jerking free the heavy

gun he wore on his hip. As the horse
drew level with him Bodie reached
up, caught hold of the stocky man's
gunhand, and yanked him out of the
saddle. A startled cry burst from the
American's lips. He hit the ground
hard, on his belly, and lay gasping for
breath, dark streaks of tobacco juice
dribbling from his slack mouth. Over
the back of the stocky man's horse,
Bodie glimpsed the man's partner. He
had his horse turned towards Bodie,
and a long-barrelled handgun filled his
palm. Moving to his left Bodie slipped
his own Colt out, thumbing back the
hammer. He dropped to one knee a
split second before the other man fired.
The bullet whacked the ground a foot
in front of Bodie. Then his own gun
returned the fire. The bullet caught the
American under the chin, driving up
through the skull, spreading on impact.
It blasted off the top of the man's
skull and a gout of blood and brains
filled the air. The rider went limp, his
lifeless body flopping noisily from the

back of his horse. Out of the corner of his eye Bodie spotted the stocky man climbing to his feet, reaching for the gun he'd dropped. Bodie rose to his feet, turning in the process, and drove his left boot into the side of the stocky man's head. He heard something crack and a second later blood spurted from the man's nose. He lost interest in the gun as he clutched both hands to his injured face.

"Hey, Bodie, leave something for me," Lon pleaded. He was leaning against the wall surrounding the well, his rifle aimed at the Mexican.

"You going to shoot him?" Bodie asked. He didn't really care if Lon did or not.

Lon shook his head. "I don't think so. Be a shame to spoil that fancy outfit."

"Ain't give it much thought." Bodie walked to the Mexican's horse. He took the man's rifle and handgun. "You won't be needing these, *jefe*," he said, and tossed them into the well.

He didn't fail to notice the expression on the Mexican's face as the silver revolver vanished from sight; it was obvious that the Mexican had prized the weapon greatly, and losing it hurt more than stopping a bullet.

"I will remember your face, *gringo*," the Mexican said coldly.

"Suit yourself, feller," Bodie said. "Now pick up your friends and get the hell out of here!"

The dead man was hauled face down over his saddle. The stocky man, still covering his bloody face, eventually managed to mount his horse. Stiff-faced with anger the Mexican returned to his own saddle.

"Tell your Don Castillo why we didn't fancy to visit," Bodie said. "Next time he ought to say please."

"I warn you both," snapped the Mexican. "Do not come to the estate or you will surely die! What you have done here today marks you for death!"

"Get the hell out of here!" Lon yelled. "Before I change my mind about killing you!"

The Mexican held his ground for a few seconds longer. Then he drew up his reins and rode off. The stocky man, leading his dead partner's horse, fell in behind.

"He'll be back," Bodie said. "And next time he'll have a whole bunch to back his play."

"Sooner we leave the better," Lon said.

"They will follow no matter where we go!"

Bodie turned and found himself face to face with a Mexican dressed in the brown robes of a priest. Staring into the Mexican's dark eyes Bodie realised he was in the presence of a man who held strong convictions — perhaps too extreme for his position in life.

"Is this your village, Father?" Bodie asked.

The priest nodded. "To my eternal shame it is!"

"Hard thing to say about yourself."

"It is true. I have stood by and

watched my people being exploited and degraded — and all by the man who called himself our patron."

"Castillo?" Bodie asked, guessing.

The priest nodded. His face hardened and his eyes glittered with anger. "Don Armando Castillo! The one who calls himself a Grandee! One of the nobility. He is no more than an agent of the Devil himself! A truly evil man. As is that wild *Norte Americano* who now helps him in his schemes."

Bodie glanced at Lon. "I'm getting the feeling we've really come to the right place." To the priest he said, "This American? Is he called Kane? Preacher Kane?"

"Si! That is the one. A crazy man. He claims to walk in the shadow of God. He speaks from the bible he carries with him, declaring himself an instrument of God's wrath!"

"Did Kane and his men bring people here?" Bodie asked. "American Indians? Those we call Kiowa?"

"I do not know their tribe," the

priest said. "But there were Indians herded through the village. Kane had his men show those poor wretches to the villagers. It was his way of warning them not to go against Castillo. Any man — or woman — who does will get the same treatment as those unfortunate souls!"

"So this Castillo is mixed up in it as well as Kane," Lon said quickly.

"We seem to have found out who," Bodie agreed. "Now we need to know why, Father?"

"Yes — I know. Better yet I can show you — and also find you a place to hide. Rivera will not rest until he finds you. Killing a man who works for Castillo — even if he was an Americano — is almost worse than going against God himself!"

"Shall we go, Father?" Bodie suggested.

"Of course. Please follow me. I will fetch my burro." The priest turned. "I am Father Lucero."

"That's Lon Walker. I'm Bodie."

"Come," Father Lucero said.

He led the way across the plaza and down a narrow alley beside the church. At the rear was a small lean-to under which stood a grey burro. Father Lucero wasted no time. He untied the burro and climbed onto its back. Kicking the animal into motion he led the way out of the village, heading for the stark, sun-dried hills beyond. They rode at a steady pace for almost three hours. All the time they were pushing deeper into the barren hills. They seemed to be composed of sand and hard rock. There was very little plant life, virtually no water. Bodie found himself wondering just what a land like this would possibly offer to anyone.

When they were far into the hills Father Lucero called a halt. He indicated that they should make no noise. Leaving their horses Bodie and Lon followed the priest. He led them along a confusing trail that wound its way in and out of the jumbled maze of rocks and shrivelled brush. They finally emerged on a high ridge overlooking a deep, wide, natural basin. Father Lucero motioned them to keep down. When Bodie looked down into the basin he realised why.

The floor of the basin seethed with activity. Lines of shuffling figures went about various tasks, overlooked by armed Mexican and American guards. There were more guards moving around the perimeter of the basin. The main activity was taking place in and around the entrance to a tunnel cut into the west side of the basin. Here there was also a short length of track laid and a constant stream of metal trucks flowed out of the tunnel, their contents being tipped onto a heap at the tracks' end.

"A mine," Bodie said. "A goddam mine! What is it, Father. Gold?"

Father Lucero shook his head. "Not gold. Silver. Tons of it buried in these hills. I have heard it said that this particular vein is one of the richest ever found in this area."

"Is this what Kane brought my people here for?" Lon asked bitterly. "To be used as slaves?"

"Si! There was no way that Castillo could get the labour he required by normal means. Too many around here have heard of his brutality. Many simply moved away. So Castillo devised a simple plan. He used Kane and his men. Sent them out to find labour. Castillo does not pay them and feeds them just enough to keep up their strength. That is why he uses only the young and the fit. Also the young women provide . . . free entertainment for the guards."

Bodie glanced at Lon. The Indian's face was lowered, his eyes searching the ground at his feet. He was experiencing his own hell at that moment and no amount of words was going to make it any easier for him.

"Those poor people have a simple choice," Lucero said gravely. "They either work or they die."

"Seems likely they'll die anyway,"

Bodie said. "The way they're being treated ain't intended to keep a man healthy for long."

"It is not. The only law down there is the law of the whip and the gun. The people work until they drop. If one dies another is put in his place."

"You mind if we get out of here?" Lon asked.

Father Lucero glanced at him, then shifted his gaze to Bodie. There was deep compassion in the priest's eyes.

"Come," he said. "I will take you to a safe place."

They returned to the horses. Now they rode higher into the hills, approaching the very peaks. Two hours' riding brought them to a narrow cleft in a high rock face. They dismounted at the priest's request and led their horses into the cleft. There was just enough room to pass along. They followed its erratic course for almost a quarter of a mile before emerging into a hidden canyon. It was the kind of place that proliferated in this kind of landscape.

They were plentiful — if a man could find them. This was their attraction; the fact that they were difficult to locate. Once a man found such a place he had a permanent refuge, a place where he could hide from the world. This particular canyon was especially attractive. The high sides kept out the wind and also any potential invader. There was a clear stream of water that originated somewhere deep in the rock, pushing its way to the surface through a wide split in the rock face. The constant supply of water kept the nearby earth in good condition, and grass had sprouted along the banks of the stream. There were a few trees too. Close by the stream, in the shade of a stand of timber, stood a solid-built cabin. It was part-adobe, part-timber, a structure built to last.

By the time Bodie and Lon had tended to their horses smoke was rising from the cabin's chimney, and soon after that the aroma of hot coffee drifted outside.

"That smells good," Lon commented.

"I hope his cooking's as good," Bodie said.

"Bodie, a man could find his peace in this place. Don't you reckon?"

Bodie shrugged. Peace was an elusive thing — something he'd had little chance to savour. It showed itself briefly, tempting, offering, and just as a man was beginning to accept, it drifted away, leaving him stranded.

The cool, shaded interior of the cabin was welcome after the cloying heat outside. There was only the one room, with a hardpacked floor and a crude open hearth against one wall. Furnishings were sparse, obviously constructed on the spot, from materials found within the confines of the canyon.

"I built this place myself many years ago," Father Lucerio informed them. "In these troubled times even a man of God sometimes needs a stronger sanctuary than such a public place as a church."

Lon put his rifle and saddlebags down. "It's a fine place, Father. How many others know of it?"

Father Lucero lifted a coffee pot off the fire. "You are the first I have ever shown this place."

"That's showing faith," Bodie muttered.

"Not really," Lucero said. "After what I saw today I do not think I have anything to fear from you."

"Maybe not from us," Bodie said. "But what about this Castillo? And Preacher Kane? They get to hear you're hiding us, it might turn rough, Father."

"Si. This I know. However, I have stood back for too long. Castillo has gone too far this time, and he must be stopped. I will shirk my responsibilities no longer."

They sat at the crude table and Lucero served the simple meal he had prepared.

"Father, what does Castillo want with all this silver?" Bodie asked.

"His need rises from ambition. Don Armando Castillo is no longer content

76

with his station in life. The life of a Grandee, ruling an empire of cattle and land, is not enough. Castillo has political ambitions, and he is a very determined, ruthless man. There are no lengths to which he will not go. First a post in the government. Then perhaps a governorship. Who knows, maybe he imagines himself as President one day. But whatever heights he chooses to ascend, he will need great wealth. There will be favours to buy, bribes to be paid, people to be manipulated. Our politics are reduced to such levels. It is a dirty business, but one in which I fear Armando Castillo will fare very well. It is a well known fact that he has little discretion when it comes to achieving a desired goal."

"So the silver is just a means to an end?" Bodie said.

Father Lucero nodded. "I am afraid so. The silver means wealth, and the more wealth a man has the higher he can climb. It is supposed to be the will of the people which elevates a man to public office. Unfortunately it appears that money can do the same for him. More often than not it can do it quicker, and can also keep him there. Once a man like Castillo is inside the political fence he is in a position to establish himself, to gain more power, to align himself with the right people — though they will be people who will only help him gain greater power. It is a sad state of affairs. As if Mexico does not already have enough trouble."

"He's going to be a hard man to stop," Lon said.

"We'll figure a way," Bodie told him.

Lon glanced across the table. "We? I thought you were just out to grab Kane and his bunch for the bounty?"

"Yeah," Bodie agreed. "So did I."

"But . . . ?"

"You quit lookin' at me like that, feller," Bodie scowled. "I just figure we might as well see this through. Like I said before — last thing I need is you playin' your own game. We'd end up shootin' at each other. So we tie both ends together and make us one big loop. If it works out — you get your people out and I get Kane and his bunch."

Lon smiled quickly. "Sure, Bodie." He refilled his mug with coffee. "All we have to do now is figure out how to do it!"

"Maybe that won't be as hard as you think," Bodie said.

7

"WE'VE looked at Castillo's setup and there ain't any way we're going to walk into that place to get your people out, Lon."

Lon glanced at the manhunter. "Agreed."

"I figure the next best thing is for Castillo to let them out for us!"

For a moment Lon was silent. He glanced across at Father Lucero, then back at Bodie. "You sure you ain't been sittin' in the sun too long?" he asked. "Are you saying that we ride to Castillo's ranchero and ask him nice if he'll let my people go?"

"Not just like that," Bodie said. "We do something else first."

"What?"

Bodie turned to Father Lucero. "What is it that's closest to Castillo? The one thing he couldn't bear to lose?"

"Armando Castillo has only two loves in his life," the priest said. "One is his daughter. When Castillo's wife died some years back he devoted his life to his daughter Victoria. It is said he will kill any man who dares to look upon her. And this I believe."

"And his other obsession is his silver," Bodie said. He turned to Lon again, catching the gleam in the Kiowa's eyes.

"Clever son of a bitch," Lon murmured.

"It was the silver I was going on," Bodie said. "I hadn't expected the girl. But she makes it better. And a damn sight easier to grab than a whole lot of silver!"

"Am I to understand that you intend to abduct the daughter of Armando Castillo?" Father Lucero's voice expressed his concern.

Bodie nodded. "If we can do it, Father."

The priest stared at him. "You have

placed me in a most compromising position, my son."

Lon placed a huge hand on the priest's arm. "Father, I understand how you feel. We're grateful. But this has to be done. It's one life against many. Not that we intend to hurt the girl."

"Father, we need something to bargain with," Bodie pointed out. "Something Castillo can't afford to lose."

"I see your reasoning," Lucero said. "Even so I cannot bring myself to approve. But I will not stand in your way. Nor will I speak of it to any other. I will return to the village, and I will pray for you both. I will also pray for Victoria Castillo. You may use this place for as long as you need."

"One thing, Father," Bodie said. "We'll need some help. Do you know where we might be able to hire some men? Half a dozen who can use a gun?"

"For what purpose?"

"To create a diversion. If we can

place some men overlooking the mine and get them to make a hell of a noise Castillo is going to get worried over his silver. Hopefully he'll get worried enough to send men from his ranchero to help those at the mine. If he does it'll give Lon and me a chance to get inside the house for a try at the girl."

"There is a place to the north. Nothing more than a trading post and a waterhole. It is called Xanatlan. You will find the men you need there. But I warn you, my friends, beware. Xanatlan is a gathering place for the lowest of the low. Men who will kill because they have nothing else to do."

"Sounds right," Bodie said.

As they prepared to leave Bodie caught Father Lucero's eye.

"Will it be safe for you in the village now?"

"If I wish safety, my son, I would not be a priest in this wild country. Thank you for your concern, but where I walk God walks with me."

"Yeah? Well pardon me for saying

it, Father, but your God ain't going to stop a bullet that's coming for you!"

Father Lucero smiled at the big, grim Americano. He knew the risks involved in returning to the village. If any of Castillo's men had seen him leave with Bodie and the Indian, then he would be in danger. Not that he worried over that. His concern was for the people of the village. He was their strength. When they needed words of comfort it was he who provided them. They were his children and had to be protected. Soon there would be a difficult time to face. There would be gunfire and violence and maybe even death. His place was in the village, with his people.

When they had left the canyon Father Lucero pointed out the way to Xanatlan.

"We'll maybe see you soon, Father," Bodie said. "*Buenos tardes*."

The trail took Bodie and Lon across the hills and down the far slopes. Riding at a steady, mile-eating pace, they covered a good distance before darkness forced them to a halt. They made a cold camp, chewing on strips of dried beef, washing it down with water.

"What gave you the idea, Bodie?" Lon asked.

"Remembered how we fooled that Yaqui. Baited him and when he bit I dropped him. We use the same move on Castillo. Make him think the business is at the mine, and once his back's turned we move."

"Bodie, you're a sneaky bastard. Smart — but sneaky!"

They reached Xanatlan an hour before noon the next day. It was a dismal place, a ragged collection of stone and adobe huts set down on an empty plain. The rain and wind of countless years had eaten away at the buildings, leaving them scarred and pitted. Xanatlan looked old, even by Mexican standards. It also looked deserted. There didn't seem to be anyone about when Bodie and Lon rode in. A window shutter, wood turned grey with age, swung to and fro on creaking hinges, moved by a hot breeze coming in across the flat plain that also brought hissing curtains of fine dust that rattled against the sides of the huts.

Bodie reined in, glanced at Lon, and shrugged.

"Come on then you bastards! Show your ugly faces! Or did I hear wrong and this place is full of old women!" Bodie's voice boomed out across the silence, faded, and was replaced by the low moan of the wind.

Then: "Who are you to disturb our peace? Speak! And be careful what you say this time!"

Bodie glanced in the direction of the challenge. In the door of one of the huts stood a broad-shouldered Mexican. He had long black hair and a drooping mustache. There was open hostility in his brown eyes and a cocked gun in his right hand.

Bodie climbed down off his horse and strode over to the man.

"Name's Bodie. I'm looking for some men who're good with guns. I come to the right place?"

"Perhaps," the Mexican said. He glanced beyond Bodie to where Lon sat his saddle. "If it was true what would you be wanting these men for?"

"A child's job," Bodie said. "One that your mother could do."

"Then why come to us?" the man asked. "You should have asked my mother first."

Bodie smiled thinly. "You were highly recommended."

The Mexican rubbed his jaw. "What is this work?"

"I need someone to act as a decoy. To create a diversion."

"So. And while this . . . diversion . . . takes place you will be doing something else?" The Mexican waited for an answer. He got none. Curiosity drew him outside the hut, his arms folded across his chest. The gun was still in sight, still cocked. "And the price?"

"When the job is over — all the silver you can carry," Bodie told him.

The Mexican's eyes shone with unconcealed greed. "Silver? Do not joke with me, *gringo*. You do not look like a man who could own so much wealth."

"I don't. But I know where to get it."

The Mexican studied Bodie for a time. He glanced over his shoulder, back inside the hut, then leaned closer to Bodie. "I think we could all talk better over a jug of *pulque*," he suggested.

"So do I," Lon said. He dismounted and joined Bodie.

"I thought you didn't drink?" Bodie asked.

Lon smiled. "Once in a while I let myself taste the evil stuff — just to remind me of the whiteman's weaknesses."

The hut was long and low. Tables and chairs were scattered about the earth floor and at the far end was a wooden counter. Xanatlan might have lacked some of the everyday amenities, but it boasted an adequate cantina. As Bodie moved across the floor he became aware of the smell hanging heavy in the air: a mingled odour of sweat and liquor. He was aware too of the eyes that watched his every move. There were close to a dozen Mexicans seated around the cantina. Every one of them carried a gun, many of them sporting a pair of revolvers. Dark, hostile faces turned towards Bodie, earthy hardness reflected in the weathered features. Bodie remembered what Father Lucero had said about the men of Xanatlan; one look at the faces in the cantina and he knew damn well that they were capable of anything.

They sat at a table. The Mexican called out and a jug of *pulque* was brought. Three glasses were banged down on the stained table. The Mexican poured the pale drink.

"What do you think of Armando Castillo?" Bodie asked.

The Mexican's face hardened. "Castillo is a pig! He wants everything and expects the world to live by his word of law! He is a man without pity or honour! He calls himself a Grandee, but he acts with the mind of a savage!"

"You crossed paths with him before?"

The Mexican pushed back his seat and stood up. He unbuttoned his shirt and stripped it off. He turned his back towards Bodie, exposing the mass of criss-cross white scars that marked his flesh.

"Look at them, Bodie! Look well and remember!"

He turned round, pulling his shirt back on. Sitting down he refilled his glass and took a long swallow. It was as if he were trying to wash away a bad memory.

"Two years ago some of Castillo's riders caught me crossing his land. All I was doing was shortening my journey. They took me to Pueblo Diablo and tied me to the whipping post. Castillo himself began the beating. They whipped me for three hours and left me to hang there overnight. The next day they hung me over my saddle, roped me in place and set my horse loose. When I finally returned to Xanatlan it took me many weeks to recover. They say I screamed in my sleep for many nights. The pain is gone now, but I carry the marks still. Nor am I the only one to suffer at Castillo's hands. Most of the men here have suffered because of Armando Castillo. Many others are dead." The Mexican filled his glass again, staring across the table at Bodie. "Tell me what you want, *amigo*, and you shall have it! To go against Castillo is my pleasure!" He held out a hand to Bodie. "I am Elfego Rojhas."

* * *

Concealed behind the ridge overlooking Castillo's mine, Elfego Rojhas and the six men he'd picked to accompany him

91

listened as Bodie outlined his plan for the last time.

At the back of Bodie's mind was the nagging thought that the whole scheme depended on Castillo sending his men from his ranchero when the shooting started. If he didn't it would all be wasted. But right now it was their best chance, and if Armando Castillo was as fanatical about his silver as all the talk implied, then he *would* send his hired guns.

Rojhas turned and grinned at Bodie. "We are ready, Bodie," he said. "If my day goes well I might even get to kill a few Castillo men!"

"I'm damn sure you will," Bodie said.

He and Lon mounted up and moved off. They rode in a wide loop that would take them away from the mine and bring them to Pueblo Diablo from the rear.

Elfego Rojhas had explained about Castillo's virtual fortress of a town. The place had once been a Spanish settlement, a town built around a great hacienda. Now it was Castillo's own town, housing his workforce and his hired guns. A walled-in town overlorded by Castillo himself — and the place Bodie and Lon had to infiltrate.

Bodie had allowed two hours. In that time he and Lon had to be in position, ready to take Victoria Castillo out from under the guns of her father. Two hours — which would bring them to noon — the time Elfego Rojhas and his men started their diversion.

The ride was long and slow. The heat and the dust made it uncomfortable, and Bodie was beginning to think he'd never see the inside of a bathtub again. He felt as if he hadn't washed for weeks, and he was already sporting a thick mass of stubble across his face.

An hour before noon Bodie and Lon drew rein in a stand of trees overlooking the town of Pueblo Diablo.

"What was it you were saying?" Lon asked. "We just slip inside, grab the girl, and slip out again." He scratched his nose. "Indeed this is great magic of white brother!"

"Balls!" Bodie muttered. "Come on, you loco Indian, and see how it's done."

They spent the next half hour circling the walled town, keeping to the thick scrub, until they reached a spot along the west side. Here they found a place where the land fell away into a dry creek bed. Dismounting, they tied their horses.

"According to Rojhas, Castillo's hacienda backs up to this section of the wall," Bodie said. "Let's hope he knows what he's talking about."

They worked their way to the base of the wall, flattening themselves against the crumbling granite. The wall rose to a height of about twelve feet, green moss sprouting from the joints of the massive stone blocks.

"Let's go," Bodie said.

Lon stood up, facing the wall, leaning against it with his hands. He didn't even blink when Bodie climbed up onto his wide shoulders. Reaching up, Bodie gripped the top edge of the wall and dragged himself up, using the rough joints between the stone blocks as footholds. Peering over the top he checked that it was clear. He waved a hand in Lon's direction and the Kiowa tossed up his coiled rope. Bodie caught the end and wrapped it round his waist, bracing himself as Lon began to climb. Together they lay on the wide ledge on top of the wall and looked down into the grounds of the sprawling hacienda.

They were above a garden thick with trees and shrubbery that shaded the silent place. Here and there flowers bloomed in splashes of brilliant colour. Their scent was heavy in the still air. Beyond the garden stood the house itself. It was an amalgam of stone, wood and adobe, blended together to form a building capable of housing a small army — which it possibly might, Bodie thought. There was no basic shape to the place. It had started, perhaps, as a smaller structure, which over the long years and changes of ownership, had been added to and improved upon. Now it was complete — a vast, almost formless building in true Spanish style; it was solid, ornate in places, yet gave the impression that nothing could disturb its monolithic strength.

Bodie dropped down from the wall, Lon close behind him. They moved to the side of the house, losing themselves in the thick shrubbery, and waited, watching the front of the place. A wide, cobbled courtyard curved away from the hacienda, flanked by trees. High, scrolled iron gates opened out onto a curving drive that led down to the central plaza of Pueblo Diablo.

The distant sound of gunfire reached Bodie's ears as flat, brittle cracks. First there were only a few ragged volleys, then over the next few minutes the shooting built up into a steady, almost precise fusilade.

Lon glanced at Bodie. "For a Mexican that ain't bad timing!"

They sweated out the next ten minutes. Bodie watched the front of the house with mounting frustration. What the hell was Castillo playing at? Did he intend to stay where he was?

Abruptly men began to appear from the house. Horses were brought. Rifles flashed in the sunlight. Orders were shouted back and forth. Bodie noticed there were a lot of white faces among the dark Mexicans. Preacher Kane's bunch!

"There's that feller Rivera," Lon pointed out.

Bodie had already spotted the man. But he was more interested in the man alongside Rivera. He knew somehow that he was looking at Don Armando Castillo himself; there was a manner in which he sat the saddle of his big black horse which spoke of his heritage. He was in his mid-forties, thick hair streaked with grey. Yet there was a strength in the high-boned face that even age couldn't mar. It was the face of arrogance, of a highborn Grandee. It was also the face of cruelty — the face of merciless dedication to his own ambition.

"You figure that's Castillo?" Lon asked.

"Well, it ain't the stableboy!"

They watched the group of riders sweep out of the courtyard and through the open gates.

"You set?" Bodie asked.

Lon nodded. They ran for the rear of the hacienda, crossing the garden again. A narrow path led them to a stone-slabbed terrace. Beneath a curving arch a wide doorway revealed a long room. It was dominated by a great dining table around which stood a couple of dozen chairs. The white walls were hung with paintings and from the ceiling swung glittering chandeliers. They crossed the room, making for the door that led into the main house. Bodie paused in the doorway, checking the way ahead. A wide passage lay in front of them, with countless doors leading off. At the far end of the passage was a large reception hall. Bodie moved quickly along the passage, Lon keeping an eye on their rear. Their boots clicked loudly on the tiled floor. Bodie wondered how many of Castillo's men were still in the house; he knew the man wouldn't take his whole force with him.

His deliberations were interrupted by a sudden movement off to his left. Bodie spun round, his Colt raised and ready to use. He found himself face to face with a young Mexican dressed in spotless white cotton. The Mexican took one look at Bodie and Lon and made to run. Bodie caught the scared look in his eyes, and reached out to grab hold of the man's arm. He jerked the Mexican round, slamming him back against the wall, then rammed the muzzle of the big Colt into the man's taut stomach.

"Senorita Castillo?" Bodie snapped.

The Mexican's eyes widened and he moaned softly. The moaning stopped when Bodie clipped the man alongside the jaw with the barrel of the Colt.

"Senorita Castillo, feller! And quick!"

The Mexican pointed across the hall to a wide staircase leading to the upper floor. Bodie shoved him in front, forcing the man up the stairs. On the landing they were faced with more passages. Bodie prodded the Mexican with the muzzle of the Colt and the terrified man led them along one passage, bringing them to high double doors.

"Senorita Castillo!" The Mexican croaked the name, indicating the door with a trembling hand.

"Gracias!" Bodie said and laid the barrel of his Colt across the Mexican's skull. Before the man had hit the floor Bodie had turned to the doors, putting his shoulder to them.

The big doors swung open. Bodie and Lon stepped inside the room, and came face to face with the daughter of Don Armando Castillo.

8

EVEN in the heat of the moment, knowing that time was something they didn't have, Bodie found himself pausing to take a long look at Victoria Castillo. He hadn't thought much about her physical appearance. Now there was no way of avoiding it. Her beauty was breathtaking; jet black hair that reached her waist; angry dark eyes that revealed the proud spirit burning in her lithe, slim, yet full-breasted young body. He caught a quick impression of a sensuous mouth in the smooth oval of her face, the red lips parting to reveal neat white teeth — and then she had turned away and was running across the room to an open window.

Bodie went after her, reaching out to catch hold of her arm. He yanked her away from the window, feeling her resistance. She spun round, yelling something in rapid Spanish. Her free hand clawed at his face, long nails tearing his cheek. Bodie swung her away from him, the force of the movement sending her face-down across the wide bed, long legs bared as her dress rode up. She rolled as she hit the bed, trying to reach the far side, failing to see Lon. He stepped in close as she came to her feet, swinging one big hand, with a deceptively easy motion. It caught her across the side of her fragile jaw and she folded back onto the bed and lay still.

"Pick her up and let's get the hell out of here," Bodie said, making for the door. Lon swung Victoria Castillo over one shoulder and loped after the manhunter.

They reached the stairs and started down. Without warning a figure stepped into view from behind a pillar on the far side of the hall below. Bodie saw an angry dark face turned up towards him. Then a gun rose, exploding with a heavy sound, powder smoke wreathing the muzzle. The bullet clipped Bodie's left sleeve in passing, tearing a splinter of wood from the stair higher up. The man ran across the hall, heading for the stairs, firing as he came and yelling in Spanish.

"Damn!" Bodie cursed. He ducked in towards the stair rail, swinging his Colt round. One foot slipped on the polished stair and he slammed up against the rail, grunting at the pain. He triggered a shot at the approaching man without aiming. His bullet screamed off the tiled floor, leaving a long white scar behind. The closeness of his shot made the man pull back a fraction. It gave Bodie a chance for a second shot. This time he took a moment to aim. His bullet ripped open the man's left side, just above the hip. Blood and bits of flesh burst from the man's ripped shirt. He twisted to the floor, dragging himself across the tiles, leaving behind a slimy trail of dark blood.

"Move it, Lon!" Bodie yelled.

They clattered to the bottom of the stairs and ran across the hall, making for the passage that would take them out of the house.

Now they could hear voices and the hammer of running feet.

Two men appeared from one of the side passages. They were both Americans. Bodie recognised one of them as the stocky, tobacco-chewing gunman from the village; the man's face still bore the marks of the encounter. As the stocky man lunged at Bodie there was the sound of a shot. It had come from Lon's rifle. A man screamed. Then a writhing shape struck the wall, slithering loosely towards the floor. The white wall suddenly bore a glistening smear of red. There was no more time to look as the stocky man smashed into Bodie. The manhunter almost went down. He saw the dull gleam of a knife in the man's hand. Bodie drew back, sensing the blade cutting through the air. He twisted to one side, his body protesting against the violent movement. The top of the blade sliced through his shirt, biting into his flesh; a sharp burst of pain streaked across Bodie's shoulder and chest and he felt the warm slickness of flowing blood ooze down his body. Bodie lunged forward while the stocky man was still trying to regain his balance. The heavy Colt smashed down across the man's face. Bone cracked and blood dappled the flesh. The man gasped, his free hand reaching up to touch his injured face. Bodie shouldered him back a step, jamming the muzzle of the Colt against the man's body. He pulled the trigger, dogged back the hammer and fired a second time. The heavy bullets ripped the man's body open, pulverising his internal organs, then blasted their way out through the small of his back in a hideous welter of blood and pulped flesh. The man catapulted across the hall, his body squirming. He cried out once before his body struck the floor and then lay twitching in a spreading pool of his own blood.

Lon was halfway across the garden area by the time Bodie burst out of the house. Dropping Victoria Castillo ungraciously to the ground Lon helped Bodie gain the top of the wall. Then he picked up the unconscious girl and lifted her over his head. Bodie swung down from the top of the wall, caught the girl around the shoulders and hauled her up beside him. Then he dropped the rope for Lon. As the Kiowa reached the top of the wall figures emerged from the house and began to fan out across the garden.

Bodie loosed off a couple of shots and saw one man go down, clutching his hands over his throat.

"Get the girl down," Lon said. He picked up his rifle and began to pick off the men down below.

Bodie swung Victoria Castillo over the wall, lowered her as far as he could and then let her drop. She landed limply, rolling down the dusty bank. Bodie followed her, landing lightly. Jamming his Colt in its holster he swung the girl up in his arms and started down the bank, yelling for Lon to follow him. The Kiowa was only a few yards behind when Bodie reached the horses.

Bodie climbed into the saddle and Lon lifted Victoria Castillo up to him. They rode along the dry creek bed for a way, then cut off across country. They picked up the trail they'd made on the way in and made for the distant hills. The place known as Pueblo Diablo fell away behind them.

Late afternoon found them deep in the rocky hills. Silence lay around them. There was nothing to see or hear. No gunfire. No pursuit from Pueblo Diablo. Bodie didn't bother to wonder why; he concentrated on getting them away from the town. It was a reasonably easy thing to do. There was enough rock about to enable them to pass without leaving much in the way of tracks behind.

Victoria Castillo had recovered from Lon's punch on the jaw. She sat upright on Bodie's horse, forced to hold onto him because her wrists had been tied. She said nothing and appeared to be ignoring both Bodie and Lon. After watching her for a while Bodie realised that she was closely studying their line of travel. He grinned to himself. She was intelligent as well as beautiful. A dangerous combination. He figured she would bear watching.

When they took time to rest the horses Bodie mentioned what he'd seen the girl doing.

"I don't want to give her the chance to figure out the route to the cabin," he said.

Lon took off his handkerchief. "Use this," he said.

★ ★ ★

"It ain't much, Senorita, but it's all we got!" Bodie said as he took off the blindfold.

Victoria Castillo scowled at him as she took a distasteful look around the

108

crude cabin, her face mirroring her thoughts.

"Where are we?" she demanded in perfect English. Her tone was that of someone well used to giving orders and having them obeyed.

"You'll be told only what you need to know," Bodie said. "And where you are ain't one of them. So just sit tight and do as you're told!"

Victoria Castillo stared at him in shocked silence. She watched him as he removed the rope from her wrists. The moment the rope slipped away she swung her right arm, her slim hand delivering a hard slap across his face. There was force behind the blow and it rocked Bodie's head. He stared at the girl for a moment, his anger rising as he caught the gleam of triumph in her dark eyes. He allowed her to enjoy it for a moment longer, and then raised his own hand and returned the slap. Victoria Castillo stepped back, a hand clapped to her burning cheek, a shine of tears now showing in her eyes. She looked wildly about her, as if she were seeking some way out, some escape that she knew was not possible. She moved away from Bodie, her shoulders sagging. Reaching the table she sat down and leaned her head in her hands.

Bodie glanced at Lon. "What the hell you grinning at?" he growled.

"Me?" Lon asked. "Not a thing. Bodie. Not a thing."

Bodie lit a fire and prepared a meal. As soon as it was ready he placed it on the table and Lon spooned it into three plates, placing one in front of Victoria Castillo. She lifted her head and stared at the food. Finally she pushed the plate away from her.

"You should eat," Lon told her, like a father talking to a sulking child. "Even if you hate us you should still eat. Didn't your father teach you the value of food?"

Victoria's eyes settled on the Kiowa's face. She was angry again. "How dare *you* speak of my father! Do you not know of his power? His influence? You will both die for what you have done today!"

"Little late for threats," Lon said. "Now eat the food, else my friend is going to be real upset."

"I would rather starve than eat food he has touched," Victoria snapped. "He is a filthy *gringo* pig!"

"Lady, you just please your damn self about the food," Bodie snapped. "You want to starve — go ahead!" His patience was wearing thin and he was fast realising that Victoria Castillo might turn out to be one hell of a pain in the neck!

"Will you please tell me something," Victoria asked suddenly. Her voice had lost its edge and her manner had softened considerably.

"Ask it," Lon suggested.

She looked from the Kiowa to Bodie. "Why have you taken me from my father?"

"We badly need something we can use to bargain with," Bodie told her.

111

"For what? Money? Cattle? Those things you could have stolen."

"People," answered Lon.

Victoria's face creased in misunderstanding. "People?"

"The Indians that Preacher Kane brought over the border to work your father's mine — we want them free!"

"But why? They are no better than the lowest peon. Their lives are of no consequence. Like the peasants they are born to be used. They mean nothing!"

For once Lon Walker had no smile, no humour in his voice. His brown face hardened visibly and for a moment Bodie had the feeling he might attack the girl. But Lon controlled his emotions.

"Senorita, those people are mine. From my tribe. They may be only peasants to you. But do not speak too lightly about them. I would not exchange one of them for a thousand of your Grandees. Because your father desires to involve himself in politics many of my tribe have been

112

slaughtered. Murdered by the animals who take your father's money!"

Victoria's face flushed hotly. Her breasts swelled with agitation as she rounded on Lon. "You lie!" she snapped. "My father would not do such a thing, and you cannot justify what you have done by accusing my father of such things!"

"It's no lie," Bodie said.

Victoria slumped back in her seat. "Why should I believe you? It could all be lies. An attempt to turn me against my father!"

Bodie moved to the stove and refilled his coffee mug. "The way you feel about your father doesn't mean a damn thing to me, lady. I want one thing. Those poor bastards being worked to death in that mine." He looked across the room at her. "You think about them, Senorita Castillo, and then remember that fancy house you live in. If you've got a God, then pray to him that you get to go back there!"

It was dark by the time they finished

their meal. Lon gave Victoria a blanket and she went over to the low cot that stood against one wall. She lay down and turned her back to them.

Lon sat down and began to clean his rifle.

"Expecting to use that thing?" Bodie asked.

Lon shrugged. "Could be. In the morning I'll take a ride down to Castillo's place. Let him know we've got his daughter — and then offer him our terms."

"You sure you want to do that?" Bodie asked.

Lon smiled. "It has to be done, Bodie, like it or not."

It was silent for a while.

Then Bodie said: "Don't trust him, Lon. Not even for a second!"

9

DON ARMANDO CASTILLO waved aside the servant filling his coffee cup as he saw the black-clad figure enter the dining room.

"Did he tell you anything, Rivera?"

"Nothing more, Patron. It was as I had expected. Elfego Rojhas has carried much hatred in his heart for a long time. It is strong enough to keep him from speaking."

There was a harsh chuckle from the other end of the table. It came from a lanky, unshaven figure hunched over a half-eaten plate of food. Bright, wild eyes stared at Rivera. Thin, bloodless lips curled back from long, stained teeth.

"That's what you get for sending a boy to do a man's job!"

Rivera's eyes flashed hotly. "You could have done better, Kane?"

"Something we might never find out now," Preacher Kane said.

"Let us not argue amongst ourselves," Castillo said. "We are faced with a difficult situation but we can resolve it."

"I should have killed those two strangers in the village," Rivera said.

Kane chuckled. "Yes, you should have — but you didn't, Rivera, an' now we are payin' for your mistake."

Rivera ignored the American. "Patron, the men are ready to ride again. We will not rest until we find those two."

"Then go," Castillo said. "My trust in you has not weakened, Rivera. I will remain here. Sooner or later we will receive a visit from one of the men who took Victoria. They have to present their demands. I wish to be here when that happens."

"What of the priest?" Rivera said.

Castillo lifted his cup and drank. "Send some men to the village, and have them bring that interfering holy man. I have a feeling he may know more of this matter. Perhaps he will become a messenger for me instead of for God!"

Rivera nodded, and with a final scowl in Kane's direction, he left the room.

"You should not taunt him so much, Kane," Castillo said.

"Ah, don't fret none," Kane grinned. "Keeps the feller on his toes if he thinks I'm belittling him. You want me to hang round? Maybe if this son of a bitch does turn up I can offer him the word." He thumped his hand down on the battered old bible he had laid on the table beside him. "The Lord will counsel my words and through me will show this transgressor the folly of his ways!"

Castillo frowned at the American. There were times when he failed to understand Kane's strange personality. The man was a good ally. When it came to a fight there was none better. Just place a different problem before him and Kane would solve it by direct or devious means. He controlled his men with an iron hand and had little regard when it came to taking life. Yet he still carried on his fanatical religious ranting, his quoting from the bible, the ever-changing attitudes that placed him out of step with everyone around him. He was, Castillo thought, a hard man, a killer, and also a man to fear because of his unstable personality.

When they had finished eating Castillo led the way outside, Kane walking at his side. They crossed to the far side of the great house, to the area where the stables and corrals stood. Castillo walked briskly to the far side of the complex.

Here he stopped, and stared in silence at the man suspended from the cross rail of the main corral gates. The man's clothing had been ripped from his body, and hung in bloody tatters. The whole of the body was a mass of bruises and lacerations. Blood had dried in dark streaks on the beaten flesh, dripped onto the dusty ground. The face was a ruined, bloody mask. Every feature hideously distorted. Flies buzzed around the swaying body, crawled over the swollen flesh.

"Such hate in a man could be channelled to great effect," Castillo said.

"Too damn late now," Preacher Kane intoned.

The blood-caked head moved. Slowly, so slowly, it raised up. One swollen eye cracked open and Elfego Rojhas stared down at Castillo.

"Praise the Lord!" Kane said. "The sinner lives!"

"Rojhas!" Castillo said harshly. "Even now you could live! Tell me what I want to know!"

"May you rot in hell!" Rojhas croaked. He groaned. Blood trickled from the corner of his mouth. "If I have caused you grief then I will gladly die!"

"Do not be a fool, Rojhas. Dying for nothing is foolish. Your friends will not carry out their plan. I will hunt them down and they will also die!"

Rojhas managed a crackling laugh. "To see you made a fool of gives me a good feeling!"

"Then make the best of it!" Castillo fumed. "A man's final hour should be enjoyable!"

Castillo turned and took Kane's big revolver from his holster. He stepped in front of Rojhas and lifted the gun, easing back the hammer.

"Do you see what I have got, Rojhas?"

Rojhas laughed harshly. "Should I care? From the moment your pistoleros killed my comrades and took me prisoner I knew I was a dead man! You cannot hurt me, Castillo, you hyena! I am already dead! So just come a little closer! Just enough so that I can piss on you from the grave!"

Castillo emptied the gun into him. Six bullets that ripped bloody holes in Rojhas's twitching body. Blood and bone and pulped flesh burst from the wounds. Rojhas's sagging mouth spat blood that dribbled down his naked chest. It dripped into the dirt beneath him, turning black as it was soaked up.

Castillo handed Kane his gun. "Thank you for the loan of your weapon," he said.

A strange smile played around Kane's thin mouth as he took the gun. He ejected the spent cartridges and reloaded the revolver. He stared at the mutilated corpse as it swayed gently at the end of the rope. His lips moved as if he was tasting some new and pleasant sensation. He moved away abruptly, falling in beside Castillo.

"This mess ain't going to sit too well with those big boys you're expecting to help you on the political wagon."

Castillo's face stiffened as if Kane's remark had caused him physical discomfort. "If I handle it well it will benefit me. But if I show weakness it will do me great harm. It is a fact, Kane, that a man who would hold office in the government must be above intimidation. There must be no sign of weakness. None at all! At any cost!"

"Then smite thy enemies and destroy them — and close thy ears to the wailing and the weeping!"

A shout reached them from the main gate of the hacienda. Castillo and Kane turned and saw a lone rider being admitted. The rider brought his horse across to where Castillo stood.

"From the look on your face I guess you know why I'm here," Lon Walker said. He climbed down off his horse, his rifle cradled in his big hands.

"You have my daughter?" Castillo asked.

Lon nodded. He glanced at Preacher Kane. The man had a half-smile on his gaunt face.

"Share the joke, feller," Lon said.

"I know why you're here," he said. Kane's eyes glittered. "You're a damn Kiowa. One of them stinkin' Indians!"

"Wait!" Castillo said. "Is this true? Is this why you have taken my daughter?

To bargain for the release of those savages?"

"For the people of my tribe, mister!" Lon yelled. "You've figured it out! Now tell me what you aim to do about it!"

Castillo smiled. "If you think I am about to release those Indians then you have wasted your time coming here. I will not make bargains with trash like you."

Lon shrugged. "You know what you stand to lose?"

"Oh, yes. My daughter. Then it will have to be. There will be no exchange."

"You bastard!" Lon yelled, his reckless temper giving way. He stepped forward and punched Castillo across the mouth, sending the Mexican to the ground. It was a bad mistake. Before Lon could recover Preacher Kane stepped up behind him, his big revolver in his hand. He lashed out with it, the barrel clouting Lon across the back of the skull. The Kiowa staggered, and began to turn towards Kane. The revolver slashed down again. It cracked down across the side of Lon's head this time — and again. Lon slumped to his knees, blood pouring down the side of his face. He felt a further blow and pitched face down in the dust.

Preacher Kane stood over him, a cold look in his eyes. He began to chuckle softly. "Oh, Lord, see how the mighty are fallen! I thank Thee for Thy deliverance! A sinner offered to my hands whom I will bring along the road of righteousness!"

10

BY late afternoon Bodie's concern began to show. He paced the cramped cabin restlessly, repeatedly going to the door to see if Lon had returned. His fear that something had gone wrong grew with every passing minute. Before Lon had ridden out in the grey light of dawn Bodie had expressed his doubts about the way Lon intended to confront Castillo.

"Bodie, how else we going to show him we mean business? The man has to know what we're up to. And this is part of the deal."

"It's a hell of a chance you're taking, Lon."

Lon had sighed. "Yeah, I know!"

Bodie wondered now if that chance had been too great. He felt trapped and helpless in the tiny cabin and the silent, hidden canyon. He had no idea what was happening beyond the high rock walls, and the lack of knowledge made the situation harder to bear.

Victoria Castillo did little to ease the situation. She hadn't spoken more than a few curt words the whole day. And her looks had a quality to them that could have killed. Under different circumstances their being together could have been a pleasant way of passing the time. Once or twice Bodie had stared at her, aware of her beauty. Her unassumed sexuality was in her every move, every expression, and never more than when she caught his stare and returned it with a dark, sullen scowl that prickled the hair on the back of his neck.

He was outside the cabin, willing Lon to show, when he heard the soft footstep behind him. Bodie glanced over his shoulder and saw Victoria standing by the cabin door. He held her gaze, and noticed that for the first time her hostility semed to have mellowed a little.

"I would like to bathe," she stated; even now her words emerged like an order. "Do you have any objections?"

"No," he said. "Long as you stay where I can see you."

Victoria's head came up, the dark eyes angry. "Do you expect me to bathe naked before you?"

"It's your choice, lady. Only I don't intend giving you the chance to even think about slipping off somewhere." He smiled without humour. "You won't be the first female I've seen without her lace pants on, so don't fret about unsettling me."

Victoria snapped at him in rapid Spanish — words Bodie didn't understand. He decided it was probably better he didn't learn what they were. She went back inside the cabin and emerged again quickly with a blanket over her arm.

"It was not your feelings I was concerned over," she said hotly.

"Well, hell, don't tell me you're turning modest all of a sudden!"

Her cheeks flamed with colour and she turned away from him, stalking off towards the stream. Bodie followed her and sat down on the ground a few yards behind her.

"Why do you not come and sit right next to me?" Victoria asked, her tone regaining its former sharpness.

"Gracias, senorita, but I'm fine right here. Don't you pay me no mind at all."

Victoria threw the blanket down on the grass. Deliberately turning her back to him she began to undress, the very act of removing her clothes a defiance of his presence. She stood finally naked, drawing her long black hair up on top of her head and tying it in place with a length of ribbon from her dress. Bodie watched her, noting that the shape hinted at by the close-fitting dress was delightfully feminine now that it had been exposed. Beneath the silky sheen of tawny flesh he could see the ripple of strong muscles playing down the long curve of her back. He caught the slight quiver of her firm, rounded buttocks as she waded into the chill water, and then she knelt and let the stream cover her to the top of her slim shoulders.

Bodie found he envied her. He felt dirty and unshaven, and it seemed a hell of a long time since he'd had a good wash. His clothing was starting to stiffen with its accumulation of dirt and sweat. He noticed his hands; they were grimed with dust, the flesh scarred and rough. He must have looked a sight. He wondered how he looked to Victoria Castillo. Like some wild animal that had just crawled out from a hole in the ground! It wasn't a bad description of how he felt right there and then. Not that he had much say in the matter. The situation he was in didn't promote an atmosphere of decency — and he didn't imagine that things were about to get any better.

The sound of splashing drew his attention back to Victoria Castillo. Avoiding his gaze she waded from the stream, water spilling from her gleaming young body. Bodie stared at her, caught by the sensual image of her nakedness, and he felt his own body ache with desire. Victoria paused at the stream's edge to scoop water up and splash it over her face. Her arms brushed against the proud thrust of her jutting, full breasts, rosy nipples erect from the cold water. Moisture glistened on the smooth torso and the flat stomach, losing itself in the thick tangle of black hair between the taut thighs. Stepping from the water Victoria snatched up the blanket and wrapped it around herself.

"Did I please you?" she asked, her voice as icy as the water in the stream.

"Better than watching the grass grow," Bodie growled.

Her features softened. So had her voice when she spoke again. "Do you want me?" she asked, leaning forward, and letting the blanket slip to expose one swelling breast.

Bodie smiled at her. "Not enough to let you go!"

"Damn you, *gringo*!" she shouted. She picked up her clothes and ran to the cabin.

Victoria had reached the door when she stopped and threw a quick glance towards the entrance of the canyon. She glanced at Bodie and saw that he too had heard the sound. It came again; the sharp rattle of stones being dislodged by a passing horse. Bodie moved to his horse and snatched his Winchester from the sheath, levering a round into the breech.

Lon Walker's horse appeared. But it wasn't Lon in the saddle. Bodie stared up into the face of Father Lucero. A face barely recognisable beneath the sheen of blood. Lucero swayed, sliding out of the saddle. Bodie stepped up and caught the priest. Father Lucero got his feet under him and regained his balance. He lifted his head and stared at Bodie. His eyes were swollen almost shut.

"What the hell happened?" Bodie demanded.

"Help me inside," Father Lucero asked. He spoke through lips badly torn and swollen.

Bodie supported the priest and led him inside the cabin, sat him down at the table. He moved to fetch water and found that Victoria had already done so. She had barely had time to pull on her dress and her hair had come loose, falling across her still-damp shoulders.

Leaving her to attend to the priest Bodie crossed to the fire and lifted the coffee pot. He filled a mug and took it to the table.

"Here, drink this," he said.

Father Lucero took the coffee, forcing it between his tender lips. As he raised the mug Bodie saw that his hands were badly bruised, the fingers thickened and crusted with dried blood. He held back his impatience, giving the priest time to drink the coffee. Draining the mug Father Lucero sat for a moment, his head bowed as if he was in prayer.

"In my life," he said, "I have seen a number of bad things. But today I have seen terrible things." He raised his head to look at Bodie. "Elfego Rojhas is dead. Butchered. Hung up on a rope like a side of beef. The men who were with him are all dead. And your friend, the Kiowa, is Don Castillo's captive!"

"Damn!" Bodie spat. It was all going wrong. The whole blasted scheme. "Why did they beat you?"

"It was the idea of that madman, Kane. A final touch to make sure you understood the message I was sent to bring you."

"Which is?"

"Castillo refuses to even consider freeing the Indians. He informed me that he will never submit to being put under pressure. His position as a Grandee does not allow for such considerations."

"The hell it don't!"

Father Lucero put a hand on Bodie's arm. "It is no use, my son. Castillo will not change his mind. He is a stubborn man."

"So am I, Father!" Bodie indicated Victoria. "What did he say about her?"

Father Lucero sighed, the sound of a man who has finally given up trying to understand his fellow creatures. "He said that you had taken her for nothing. Even though she is his own flesh he will not bargain for her."

"No! It is not true, Father!" Victoria's voice trembled, uncertainty edging her words. "Do you expect me to believe that my own father would abandon me?"

The priest reached out and took hold of her slim hands. "My child, would you expect me to lie? I will not deny that I have little liking for your father. He and I have been in conflict for many years. You have witnessed my visits to Pueblo Diablo. You have heard me plead with Don Castillo on behalf of his peons. And just as many times he has turned me away. But my words are the words of truth — of God's truth — I think you know that. Have we not respected each other over many years? Since you were a child?"

Victoria nodded quickly, turning her head away — but not before Bodie caught the gleam of tears in her eyes.

"Listen to me, Victoria," Father Lucero pleaded. "I am not here to condemn. Simply to tell what I saw. My words have given you pain and for that I am sorry. But truth has the habit of doing such things."

"Father, just what is Castillo planning?" Bodie asked.

"He will scour the countryside for you. Your friend . . . I think Castillo will kill him. Or perhaps he hopes to lure you to the hacienda in an attempt to free him." Father Lucero shrugged. "I do not know, my son. I am weary."

"Take it easy. You've earned it." Bodie made for the door. "Look after him," he said to Victoria.

"If I were to be honest, Father," Victoria said as Bodie left the cabin,

"I would have to say that I no longer know my father."

"I thought that he was devoted to you."

Victoria's smile was sad. "Only as one of his personal possessions. I was as one of his prize horses. Something to be admired. To be paraded before his guests. To talk intelligently. To play pretty tunes on the piano. To be eventually married off to the son of some other rich and influential Grandee. A means of carrying on the breed!"

"I find this hard to accept."

"Accept it, Father, for what it is. The truth! My father devotes his life to his new desire. His political career! Perhaps he has educated me too well. I am aware of his aspirations — and I realise that with the support of his powerful friends, his fortune in silver, and his ruthlessness he will easily attain his ambitions."

"Victoria, what will you do?"

"I will survive, Father. One lesson I

am grateful to Don Castillo for. If he taught me nothing else, he did teach me how to survive — and I will!"

The cabin door swung open and Bodie framed himself in the opening.

"Father, were you followed?"

Father Lucero lurched to his feet. "Followed? I thought not. I was most careful after I left Pueblo Diablo. Many times I stopped to look behind me. But I am not an expert. A skilled man could follow without my knowledge."

"Looks like it's been done," Bodie said. He closed the door. "There's someone in the brush near the entrance to the canyon."

"Castillo's men?"

Bodie shrugged. "It's for sure they ain't come neighbouring." He stood by one of the windows, his eyes searching the thick brush that lay along the canyon floor. Somewhere in that tangle of undergrowth armed men were working their way closer to the cabin.

"Have you time to get away?" Father Lucero asked.

"Maybe," Bodie said. He turned from the window, picked up his saddle bags and scooped out a box of cartridges for the rifle, tipping them into his pants pocket. "There a back way out of here?" he asked.

"There is a place at the far end of the canyon where a landslide broke the wall. I have never tried it, but I think it could be climbed. It would be hard and you could not take the horses."

"Then we leave 'em," Bodie said. "Figure you can make it, Father?"

Father Lucero smiled. "I will not be going. It is your life which is in danger. You need the chance to get away. Take it before Castillo's men come."

"Staying here could get *you* killed."

"Si. This I know. But it is a risk I am prepared to take. If you stay there will be no chance for you."

Bodie snatched up his canteen, glad he'd taken the trouble to fill it from the stream. He turned to Victoria, and found her already on her feet.

"I am ready," she said.

138

He studied her for a moment, not sure how to take her change of attitude, but not having the time to question it.

"Look out for yourself, Father," he said.

"God go with you both!"

Bodie opened the cabin door and stepped outside, drawing Victoria with him. Father Lucero's words drifted after him. The trouble was, Bodie decided, he needed a damn sight more than the help of God on his side. He could have done with Lon Walker at his back.

11

THEY moved quickly away from the cabin, cutting across open ground. Victoria needed no urging. She ran ahead of Bodie, making for the stand of timber he'd indicated. The distance was slight, but it seemed an eternity; the trees never seemed to get any nearer.

Bodie heard a man shout. He glanced over his shoulder and saw a figure near the cabin. A Mexican. Beyond him others were breaking out of the brush. More shouting. Arms waving. And then a rifle was raised and the sound of a shot drowned everything else.

Something slapped Bodie's left shoulder. He felt himself falling and it was only as he hit the hard ground that he felt the pain. It was white-hot and it burst suddenly, flooding his shoulder with agony. Sweat beaded his face. Bodie struggled to his feet. He could hear boots slapping the ground behind him and he knew he didn't have any time to spare. As he looked up he saw Victoria had turned towards him.

"Damn you, woman!" he screamed. "Keep going! You come back this way and I'll shoot you myself!"

She stopped, her face pale with either fright or anger. He wasn't sure which — but she obeyed him and turned around again.

Bodie spun, facing the advancing men. They were close enough to have faces now, and he saw that they weren't all Mexicans. There were some white faces among the brown: Preacher Kane's guns!

Bodie swung up the Winchester. His left hand seemed to be going numb, but he closed his fingers round the rifle. His fingers touched the trigger and the Winchester exploded heavily. He saw a puff of dust rise from the shirt of one of the Mexicans. The man gave a strangled yell as the bullet flipped him over onto his back, blood spouting from the hole in his chest. The back of his shirt bulged, then split, allowing a gout of red to spatter the ground. While the Mexican was going down Bodie was seeking a fresh target, triggering a deadly hail of bullets. He saw a second man go down, clutching bloody hands to a leg that was squirting blood at a terrifying rate. The other attackers split apart, making for cover. Bodie put a bullet through the back of one retreating head, bursting the man's brains out through the hole the flattened bullet made on exit.

He turned and headed for the trees, knowing that the men would be coming again soon. He caught sight of Victoria and waved her on. They weaved their way through the timber, feet making no sound on the soft ground. Bodie could feel the cold, greasy sickness rising in his stomach. Reaction was setting in. His senses were getting themselves sorted out and his body was registering the fact that he'd stopped a bullet.

The timber slipped away from them and they were in the open. Bodie pointed to where the canyon started to narrow. Above the vegetation he could see the place where the landslide had scarred the otherwise unmarked line of the canyon wall.

"How can you climb with your shoulder?" Victoria asked.

"Forget it. No time now." He caught hold of her arm, spun her round, almost dragging her along. "Move!"

The brush was higher and thicker here, much of it thorny. The sharp barbs hooked in their clothing, ripped at their flesh. At times they were forced to a dead stop as they pushed through tangled barriers of brush. Without warning the ground fell away into a steepsided, dry watercourse. They plunged down the dusty bank in a choking yellow mist. As he hit bottom Bodie heard Victoria cry out. He struggled to his feet and went to where she lay, took hold of her arm and dragged her upright. There was a bleeding gash above one eye.

"You still able to walk?" he asked.

Some of the fire still gleamed in her eyes as she brushed dark hair from her face. "Yes, I am well able to walk!"

Bodie watched her stumble her way to the rim of the far bank. He followed, his mind digesting the fact that she refused to allow her feelings over her father to drag her down.

The brush thinned out a little for them. Twenty yards up the canyon lay the crushed mass of tumbled rock left behind after the avalanche. Bodie glanced up at the high rim of the canyon wall. Father Lucero had told him it wouldn't be an easy climb; now Bodie could see why.

"All right, Senorita, up we damn well go!" Bodie said as they reached the spot.

Victoria glared at him. "Is it not possible for you to speak without cursing all the time?"

"Way I feel right now, Senorita Castillo, the answer's no!"

They started to climb, moving from rock to rock, forced to take care that whatever they stepped on would support them. There was a lot of loose shale and smaller stuff amongst the large chunks of splintered rock. More than once they disturbed loose rock, and would hear it leap and bound down the slope, freeing other rock on the way. It was this that worried Bodie. He realised that they could create another full-scale slide if they disturbed too much rock. Knowing this made the climb that much more difficult; it was just another complication to add to what they already carried.

Victoria managed to climb well, despite the encumbrance of her long dress. Bodie found it tiring, though he realised that his shoulder wound was a contributing factor. It was hurting badly now and he was still losing blood; there was a continuous trail of it across his left hand, and each time he placed his palm down on a rock he left a bloody palmprint behind.

They were well over two thirds of the way to the top when Castillo's men appeared far below. Bodie happend to be looking in that direction when they stepped into view. The moment they saw him they opened fire. Bullets whipcracked off the stones around Bodie and Victoria, screaming off into the sky. Stone chips exploded in white flashes.

Bodie turned and wedged himself against two slabs of rock. Lifting the Winchester he loosed off a couple of shots at the men below, and saw them scatter. His third shot was fired after a few moments of steady aim; the slam of the shot bounced back and forth across the canyon, and down below a man fell face down in the dust, Bodie's bullet lodged deep in the back of his skull. Bodie took the opportunity to feed fresh cartridges into the Winchester before he moved on, following Victoria.

"Tell me where we are running to?" she asked.

"Right now we're just running," he told her. "Away from those damn guns your father pays!"

He saw the familiar gleam in her eyes, noticed it fade. "A while ago I would have killed you for saying such a thing!"

"And now?"

"Now I do not know what to believe. Maybe time will answer the questions in my mind."

Bodie moved across to her, nudging her into action. "Trouble is we don't have any time to spare right now. That bunch down there ain't about to hold off while we sit a spell . . . so let's go!"

They slipped and clawed their way up the rock slide. The harsh stone tore at their clothing and their flesh. Progress was slow and as they moved up the bare layers of rock they were acutely aware of how exposed they had become.

Shots rattled below them. Bullets struck the rock around them, above them, and below them, as Castillo's men tried to range their rifles.

"We are almost there!" Victoria said jubilantly.

Bodie didn't answer. He was watching the men far below. They had started to climb the rocks.

"Only a few more feet," Victoria called. "Bodie — are you listening?"

He waved her on. Glancing back Victoria saw what was holding his attention. She pulled herself up the last few feet and rolled onto the canyon rim. Peering over the edge she saw that Bodie had laid aside his rifle and was pushing at a large slab of rock balanced near the top of the slide. A great part of the rock lay unsupported, and as Bodie put his weight against it the rock tilted. It hung for a moment, suspended, and then it slid away from Bodie, grating against the rock beneath it. Its own bulk turned it over and over as it dropped. It struck the slide, bounced heavily, and then carried on rolling, drawing more and more rocks and debris with it. A pale wreath of dust misted the air in its wake as it crashed on down towards the canyon floor, and behind came an increasingly larger avalanche of rock. A low sound, like distant thunder, filled the air. A thick cloud of dust hid the canyon floor from sight and as the hurtling, bounding slabs of stone smashed to the canyon floor far below, a single, shrill scream rose — a brief sound that was soon lost in the heavier roar of falling rock.

Neither Bodie nor Victoria stayed to see the result of the fall. They moved quickly across the wide rim of the canyon, searching for a way that would lead them down to the comparative smoothness of the flatlands below.

By the time they had worked their way to the base of the high canyon wall it was getting dark. Bodie spotted a shallow cave beneath a rocky overhang and they crawled inside. The cave broadened and heightened beyond the entrance. It was sparse, inhospitable and cold, but in their exhaustion it offered at least a degree of comfort and protection.

"Before it becomes too dark for me to see," Victoria said, "let me look at your shoulder."

Bodie made no argument this time. His shoulder, though it had stopped bleeding, still hurt. His arm was stiff and he was feeling weak from the loss of blood. At Victoria's insistence he sat down and allowed her to remove his shirt. He caught her gazing at the scars marking his body.

"I fall down a lot," he told her dryly, and for the first time he saw a smile touch the corners of her soft mouth.

"I think also that you tell many lies!" She took the canteen and uncapped it. Tipping water onto her hands she washed and rinsed them. Bodie watched as she tore a strip of material from her underskirt. "You are very lucky, Bodie," she said. "The bullet has come out. I will clean the wound and bind

150

it. There is nothing more I can do for now."

Bodie sat in silence as she worked, filling his mind with thoughts to blot out the pain. He was thinking about Lon Walker, wondering how the Kiowa was — if he was still alive. Damn! The whole thing had turned into one hell of a mess. Rojhas was dead. He didn't know whether Lon was alive or not. And he was stuck out in the middle of nowhere with a hole in his shoulder and a girl on his hands. He began to wonder if any eventual bounty he might pick up would be worth all the damn trouble he was going through to get it!

Another puzzle was which side Victoria was on. Her attitude had changed considerably with Father Lucero's explanation of Don Castillo's actions. But was it only a temporary change? Was she liable to revert to her normal self? Hating the sight and sound of him! Despising him! He glanced at her, wondering.

"I think that will help," Victoria said.

Bodie snapped out of his thoughts. The light was failing fast now, the setting sun casting a rich red flood of colour across the land. Victoria's lovely face smiled at him, features softened by the sunset.

"Thanks," he said.

"What will we do now?" she asked.

Bodie pulled his shirt back on. "What we should be doing is looking for a place where we can get food and a place to sleep. I figure that's enough for tonight. You got any suggestions?"

"I can only think of one place," Victoria said. "The cabin of Tomas Silvana."

"Who is he?"

"A shepherd. He has grazed his flocks in these hills for many years. From before I was born. He is an old man. Very proud and very independent. And he does not like my father. Nor is he afraid of him. Often when I have been out riding I have stopped by his cabin

152

to talk with him. We are good friends. He would let us stay in his cabin."

"How far is it?"

"In two hours we could easily walk there."

"Well we ain't in a position to be choosy," Bodie said. "Let's just hope your shepherd stays friendly long enough for us to get some sleep."

12

"**H**ELP yourself to more food, senor!"

Bodie nodded and reached for the bowl of lamb stew on the table before him. He spooned it onto his plate, realising just how hungry he was, and there was no getting away from the fact that the stew was delicious.

"Tomas, may I have some more coffee?" Victoria asked.

"Si, Victoria."

Tomas Silvana had expressed no surprise when Bodie and Victoria had walked out of the darkness to his tiny cabin. His reaction had been one of genuine pleasure at their company, and he had welcomed them with a show of hospitality that revealed his warmth and affection for Victoria.

"And what is your intention now, Bodie, my friend?" he asked after filling

Victoria's cup. "It will not be a safe place for you anywhere. Don Castillo has a long arm, and he has influential friends."

It was Victoria who answered, putting into words the thoughts that had been filling Bodie's tired mind. "We will face my father, Tomas. There is nothing to be gained by running away. It will not solve the problem."

Silvana sat down and studied her young face for a long time. He was an old man, but he retained his sharp mind and the alertness of a much younger man. His brown face was lined, his hair white, but he missed nothing.

"This thing could be dangerous for you," he told Victoria. "It is difficult for me to speak of your father in your presence — but I would warn you to be on your guard against him!"

Victoria smiled. "I have learned many things about my father, Tomas, in a very short time. They are unpleasant things, yet they are true. If I had been more attentive I would have realised the wrong things he has been doing long ago. I am paying for that foolishness now."

"Victoria, I am sorry." Silvana laid his creased hands over Victoria's. "It is a sad fact of life that we often do not really know those we are closest to."

"Whatever happens I must face my father. I must ask him about the terrible things I have heard!"

"You really think it's the thing to do?" Bodie asked.

Victoria glanced across the small table at him. "Perhaps for the first time in my life I am doing the right thing."

Tomas Silvana sighed, sitting back from the table. "When I was very young, the world was a beautiful place in my eyes. As I grew older my eyes grew wiser, and I saw the flaws in the world and my childhood dreams were shattered. As I became old my eyes dimmed and the flaws seemed to vanish. Now I see the world as I saw it as a child. Yet I know there are bad things happening, though I will often pretend that they do not exist. It is foolishness. We live in an imperfect world. Shutting our eyes to those imperfections will not make them go away. You are right, Victoria, to face your problems. In running away from trouble you only find, that in truth, you are running towards it."

The old man stood up. He turned away from the table and picked up a battered old sombrero. He draped a blanket around his thin shoulders. From a corner of the cabin he took an ancient single-shot rifle, dropping a handful of shells in his pocket.

"We pushin' you out?" Bodie asked.

Silvana shook his head. "A wolfpack has been troubling my sheep at the grazing pasture. Tonight I will be waiting for them." He thrust bread and a portion of cheese into a leather pouch along with a squat stone jar. "Now I am ready."

"Take care, Tomas," Victoria said.

She stood up and went to him, kissing him gently on the cheek.

Silvana smiled. "After that I could kill wolves with my bare hands. Only an old man could receive such a kiss!" He lifted a hand in farewell. "Sleep well, my friends."

The door closed quietly behind him. Bodie poured himself another coffee, sat nursing it in both hands, silently watching Victoria. For no apparent reason he found he was picturing her stepping out of that cold stream, her naked young body firm and glistening, the beaded water sliding across her taut stomach into the dark hair below. She looked different now. Her dress was dirty and torn to shreds. Her thick hair lay in a tangled dark mass across her shoulders. But she still looked damn beautiful, he decided. It was a fact he couldn't deny — or want to.

Victoria moved to the table and quickly cleared it. She rinsed the dishes in the large wooden pail that Silvana kept for such a purpose. Afterwards she secured the cabin door. Reaching up she put out the oil-lamp suspended from the low ceiling. There was still enough light coming from the fire blazing in the open hearth.

"It is very late, Bodie!" she said out of the shadows.

He glanced across to where she was standing beside the bed, and even in the faint light he noticed the gentle smile touching her lips. Victoria raised her hands and began to slowly unfasten her dress . . .

Bodie stood and went to her, studying her for a moment, and then he reached out and drew her to him. Victoria's head tilted back as his mouth came down onto hers, soft lips parting, a whisper of sound coming from her throat as Bodie eased her onto the bed. Her loosened dress parted beneath his hands and Bodie felt the heated swell of her naked breasts against his palms. Victoria groaned as he explored the rising hardness of dark nipples, arching her hips against his body.

"This is crazy," Bodie said. "Tomorrow I might be trying to kill your father!"

Victoria's eyes shone in the glow of the firelight as she stared up at him. "Tomorrow is a long way away," she said softly. "Yesterday I hated the sight of you, and I would have killed *you* if the chance had come my way. Now I am sure of nothing — and who knows what tomorrow might bring! I am only certain of this moment and what I wish to do with it." She smiled suddenly, her face relaxing and her youthful beauty almost dazzling him. "We have come together, you and I, by circumstance, so we must accept the situation. Also I am curious about you, Bodie."

"Oh?"

"I offered myself to you once before and you refused me. No woman likes to be refused."

"Don't think I didn't consider it. Trouble was you chose the wrong time and place."

160

Victoria eased herself from beneath him, and Bodie watched her slip out of her clothing. Naked she turned and faced him.

"And what of this time, Bodie?" she asked.

Bodie slid his hands around her smooth hips, drawing her close. She let herself fall against him, her hands eagerly loosening his clothing.

"I figure this is as good a time as any," he said finally. Victoria gave a gentle, hissing sigh as he lowered himself against her. She curved her supple form to his, thighs sliding over him, drawing him down to where she was ready and waiting to receive him . . .

★ ★ ★

Bodie woke suddenly blinking against the brilliant sunlight streaming in through the cabin's open door, and he lay for a moment, held by the lulling comfort of the warm bed. He was tempted by a remembrance of the previous night. He sat up as he realised Victoria was not beside him. The fire had been rekindled and a bubbling pot of coffee stood over the flames. Where the hell was she, he wondered. He swung his legs out of the bed and stood up. He felt stiff and his left shoulder still troubled him. He hadn't slept all that well. The bed wasn't all that big, especially as he'd been sharing it with a restless and surprisingly energetic young woman. He pulled on his clothes, stamping his feet into his boots, wondering if last night's episode was an indication he might be getting old! He grinned. The youngest old man in the whole Southwest! He crossed to the door and stepped outside.

Victoria was standing out in the open, her back to him. She was watching two riders coming down off a distant ridge. Following behind one of the riders was a stumbling figure. A man on foot, his hands tied, and a rope around his neck leading back to the rider.

"That's the old man," Bodie said, anger rising in his voice.

Victoria turned to look at him. Her eyes were moist with tears. "See what they have done to him, Bodie!"

"You know those riders?"

"Si. Butler and Radigan. Two of Preacher Kane's Comancheros!"

Bodie stepped back inside the cabin. He picked up his rifle and the Colt.

"Maybe you ought to go inside," he suggested.

Victoria shook her head. "No! The time for walking away is past."

Bodie moved to her side. He took his Colt and pressed it into her slim hand. She took it without question, holding it so that the folds of her dress concealed it.

The riders came up the gentle rise towards the cabin. As they neared the place Bodie saw that they both held their guns in their hands. He judged Butler and Radigan for what they were — a pair of ten-to-the-dollar hired guns, the kind liable to be more vicious than professionals skilled at their trade. Even so he eyed them with caution. It only took a slip on someone's part to start trouble that could only end in sudden, violent death.

Victoria gave a shocked cry. Before Bodie could stop her she had run towards the old man on the end of the rope. Tomas Silvana looked as if he had been savagely beaten.

"Hey now, honey," one of the riders said. "I don't think you should be going near that old feller."

Victoria ignored him as she reached Silvana. She made the old man kneel down. "Why have you done this to him?" she asked angrily. "Tomas is an old man. He bothers no one. What does such a cruel beating achieve? Tell me, Radigan!"

The one called Radigan glanced at Victoria briefly, his expression one of surly indifference. "If I was you, Senorita Castillo, I would shut my mouth an' do it damn quick!"

164

"Never mind her," the other rider said. "It's him we come for!"

Radigan grinned, his teeth gleaming white against his brown, unshaven face. "You figurin' on using the rifle, mister?"

"I don't carry it to lean on," Bodie said. "Whether I use it is up to you!"

The second rider — Butler — gave a ragged laugh. He leaned across his saddle and shook his head. "Hell, he don't look all that tough to me, Joe. Dirtiest saddletramp I ever laid eyes on."

"He is more man than you could ever hope to be!" Victoria snapped, and then she flushed at Butler's knowing leer.

"Well now," he said. "Sounds like the little lady's been lifting her skirts and offering round her favours, Joe." He twisted round in his saddle. "Hey, honey, you got any left for me and . . . !"

He never completed the sentence. There was only time for a brief moment of surprise as he saw the heavy revolver in Victoria's hands, and then it exploded with sound, the hard recoil almost snatching it from Victoria's grasp. The bullet hit Butler in the throat, angling upwards through his skull, blowing flesh and bone clear as it exited. Blood gushed from the ragged hole in Butler's throat, soaking the front of his dirty shirt.

Radigan stiffened at the sound of the shot. Even as he raised his gun he glanced back over his shoulder — a purely responsive action against the sudden shot — and in doing so he gave Bodie all the edge he needed.

Bodie tilted the muzzle of the Winchester up and put two shots into Radigan's body. He heard the gunman yell, and then Radigan was falling out of his saddle, blood seeming to erupt from his torn flesh. He hit the ground on the far side of the horse, his face smashing against the ground with a meaty sound. Blood spurted from his mouth and nose. Radigan twisted in agony, one arm and hand waving uselessly in the air as his shattered nerves lost control. Bodie crouched, shooting under the horse's body, putting another bullet into Radigan's bloody body. Radigan jerked, his mouth spitting blood, and he rolled over onto his back and lay still.

Bodie moved to where Butler sat hunched on the ground. The top of the man's head was an ugly sight and Bodie saw there was no danger from the man.

He saw Victoria freeing Tomas Silvana from the ropes. The old man spotted Bodie and smiled through the dried blood caking his face.

"Though you did not do it for me, my friend, I thank you for killing those two," he said.

Bodie helped the old man to his feet. "They needed killing," he said, then glanced across at Victoria. "You all right?"

She nodded, but he could see the scared look in her eyes. "Don't think about it," Bodie told her. "They were working up to killing somebody. We just got to it first."

Inside the cabin they got Silvana seated at the table. While Bodie got the old man a drink Victoria began to doctor the old man's battered face.

"I am sorry I almost caused you to be caught," Silvana said.

"Hell, we should be sorry for getting you involved."

"You will still go through with what you decided last night?"

Bodie nodded. "Yeah. Sooner or later our luck's going to run out if we keep running. And I can't just walk away with Lon Walker in trouble."

Silvana sighed. "If I were a younger man I would gladly go with you!"

"If you *were* a younger man I'd damn well take you!" Bodie said.

Victoria took the old man to his bed and got him settled down. Feeling in the way Bodie took a cup of coffee and went outside. He squatted in the dust just beside the door, his back to the cabin wall.

He stared at the dark shapes of the dead gunmen, and the darker stains of their blood on the ground. Already flies were gathering. He could hear the droning buzz of the insects. The way things were shaping up a few more would be dead before this was over.

He heard a soft sound as Victoria came out of the cabin. She knelt beside him. For a moment her gaze was held by the two bodies, then she turned her head away.

"To see death come in such a way is a terrible thing," she said. "Is it really true that such things were done to the people of Lon's village? By these wild men who work for my father?"

"Seems so."

Victoria shook her head. "You must hate my father very much."

"Never give it much thought. When I came down this way I was looking for Preacher Kane and his bunch. I didn't know they were mixed up in your father's business until later. By then I was involved with Lon and it had gone too far for me to back out."

"And now he is your enemy too."

"It's the way the cards are dealt."

"Si. This I know."

"Victoria, maybe I should go to the hacienda myself. Ain't any way of knowing what might happen when I get there."

"No! I am involved in this matter as much as you! Was it not your actions which first brought me into this terrible business? Now I must confront my father!"

"It could be dangerous."

"Any more dangerous than what we have already been through? Do you think I am afraid?"

Bodie smiled at her beautiful but angry expression. "I'll tell you the truth — I'm scared!"

"Last night you showed no fear," she said, her eyes shining with a devilish gleam. "Last night you were *muy hombre*!"

"Yeah? Well there's one hell of a difference between facing a loaded gun

170

and what you were pointing at me!"

Victoria laughed in a most unladylike manner. "It is sometimes said that a man can be more afraid of a woman than of any other thing of which he knows."

"Maybe that shows I ain't as bright as I thought I was."

"No, I do not think so, Bodie. You are a difficult man to understand — but a fool and a coward you are not!"

"We'll find out if that's true any time now," he said, and rose to his feet. "Time we got the hell out of here and paid your daddy a visit!"

Victoria followed him back inside the cabin. The thought of what lay ahead filled her with dread. The possible outcome worried her, and she found that she was more concerned over what might happen to Bodie than her father's fate. Only now did she admit to herself that she *was* frightened.

13

LON had decided during the night that come daylight he was going to make an attempt to escape from the hacienda. The longer he stayed the greater the chance he'd end up dead. He knew Don Castillo was only playing games with him. The Grandee could have him killed at the snap of his fingers. Lon had no intention of sitting back and allowing it to happen. If he had to die, let it happen while he was on his feet, making a fight of it — like a Kiowa warrior and not some toothless old man sitting in the sun just waiting for death to claim him.

He had thought of his people, too, the ones he'd come looking for. He was no damn use to them the way he was now. If they were to have any chance he had to make a try at

172

breaking free. And there was Bodie. Out there somewhere with Castillo's daughter — that wouldn't be any picnic! Between the two of them they'd stirred up some dust around Castillo — it would be one hell of a waste to allow it to settle.

Lon had checked his room over. There was only one way out — through the door. The window, which looked out over the corrals and stables, was heavily barred. The floor was cold, hard stone. So the door had to be his route out of the place. All Lon had to do was to wait for it to be opened.

That didn't happen until the middle of the morning. Lon heard the heavy bolt slide back and then the door swung open to admit the Mexican called Rivera. The passage beyond the door lay empty and clear.

"You will come with me," Rivera said. He stood framed in the doorway, his right hand close to the butt of his holstered revolver, his eyes begging Lon to try something.

His brown face impassive, Lon got up off the bed and crossed the room.

"Come quickly," Rivera snapped. "Don Castillo does not like to be kept waiting!"

"That so!" Lon murmured as he neared Rivera, and saw that the Mexican had started to lift his gun from the holster. Lon quickened his step, moving around Rivera. The Mexican twisted his body slightly so that Lon could step through the door. Lon took one more step, stopped dead in his tracks, and threw himself back against Rivera. The back of the Mexican's head rapped against the thick wood with a solid thump. Lon came round full circle, left hand reaching out to grab for Rivera's gunhand. He drove his knee up into Rivera's groin and drew a pained gasp from the man. In the same instant Lon slammed the base of his right palm up under Rivera's jaw; Rivera's teeth snapped together with a brutal crack; teeth splintered and blood spurted from between his lips.

Lon, feeling Rivera's gunhand pushing against his, turned his body in against the Mexican, closing the fingers of his right hand over the man's wrist. He began to twist. Rivera gasped and clawed at Lon's face with his free hand, drawing blood as his nails opened long, deep scratches down one side of the Kiowa's cheek. Lon ignored the pain, using the stimulation to increase the pressure on Rivera's wrist. There was a sudden crack as a bone splintered. The revolver slipped from Rivera's hand. Drawing back from the moaning Mexican Lon looped a powerful left fist round, sledging a cruel blow to Rivera's lean jaw. The Mexican spun away from the door, blood spraying from his slack mouth. He clutched the doorframe in an attempt to keep on his feet, but Lon came up behind him, plucking the slim-bladed knife Rivera carried from his belt, and with a practiced motion reached over the Mexican's shoulder and slit his throat wide open. Rivera choked on the rising flood of blood.

He slithered down the doorframe and curled up on the floor, his blood pooling around his black-clad body.

Lon picked up the revolver. He bent over Rivera and loosened the gunbelt, sliding it free from the body. He buckled the belt round his waist, then made his way along the passage, towards the door at the far end.

The door opened well before Lon reached it. A Mexican, carrying a rifle, stepped through.

"Rivera?" he called. "Rivera . . . "

Lon lifted the revolver and triggered two shots into the man's body. The impact threw the man sideways against the wall of the passage, his blood spotting the whitewashed adobe. The rifle clattered to the floor as the Mexican fell. Lon grabbed it as he stepped over the dead Mexican. He made sure it was ready for use. He knew he was going to need it now — those two shots would have the whole place on the alert!

He booted the door open. A stretch

of dusty earth lay between him and the main house. There was no hesitation in Lon's actions. He cleared the door and ran, making for the hacienda.

"Hey!"

An American appeared from over by the corrals. He had a raised gun in his hand. Behind him were two more of Kane's Comancheros.

Lon swore softly. He threw himself full length across the ground, twisting his body before he touched the earth. He rolled easily, firing as he did. His first shot caught the lead Comanchero just above the belt-buckle. The man folded over as if he was hinged. The top of his head hit the ground with a sodden thump. He was still falling when Lon's rifle crashed again. A second man went down, three bullets ripping through his chest, leaving ragged wounds in his back. The third Comanchero let himself fall to the ground, his handgun spitting flame and smoke in Lon's direction. One bullet burned across the top of Lon's left shoulder. It was the only one to touch him. Lon dropped the muzzle of the rifle, catching the Comanchero as he raised himself off the ground. The bullet drilled a neat hole in the top of the man's skull, driving down through the brain; blood spurted from the hole in the skull, while more trickled from ears and nose; the Comanchero's legs kicked spasmodically, his body tensing before it flopped limply against the bloody earth.

Lon was on his feet even as the third man was going down. He spotted other figures heading in his direction, and he knew he couldn't stand them all off. He changed direction, cutting across a dusty compound towards a wooden door set in a long stone wall. Lon's shoulder slammed against the door as his hand yanked back the heavy bolt. The door swung inwards and Lon followed it. Sunlight spilled into the room and he saw stacked wooden casks, wooden boxes and reels of what looked like white cord. A grin split his brown face. He turned, glancing back outside, and saw that the pursuing figures had halted. Some were even drawing back. Lon began to chuckle. They weren't going to follow him in here!

He moved across the small store-room. There was no other way out — just the one door. Not that it mattered. When he did leave this place it would be by the door he'd used coming in. He turned and began to inspect the casks of black powder, the boxes of dynamite, the reels holding fuse wire.

He leaned his rifle against the wall by the door. Dragging a box of dynamite from the top of the stack he used Rivera's knife to prise off the lid. The dynamite lay in neat rows, like big candles. Lon took a reel of fuse wire and cut short lengths. He'd seen the stuff in use before; it was often used on ranches to clear away stubborn trees, to blast clear fouled up streams. Working quickly he fused a dozen sticks and carried them to the door.

Putting them aside he returned for a couple of powder casks. Back by the door he peered outside. Mexican and American faces were clustered together on the far side of the compound. Lon hefted one of the casks, estimating its weight.

"Here goes nothing," he murmured softly, and hurled the cask out through the door. He watched it hit the hard ground and roll. Snatching up his rifle Lon aimed, fired, and fired again. His first bullets splintered the cask. Then he began firing at the iron bands that were bound around the cask. His hope was to clip one of the bands and cause a spark. It would only need one to ignite the powder, he hoped, then began to wonder if the idea had been such a good one as three shots failed to do a thing. He fired again, levered the rifle for another shot . . .

The compound shook as the powder exploded. There was a stunning thump of sound. A ball of flame gushed skywards, followed by a boiling mass of thick smoke. The force of the blast pushed Lon back through the door of the storeroom. The air was full of dust and splintered wood. It fell from the sky like rain. Lumps of hard earth and smouldering wood. A chunk of wood landed a few feet from the door, still smoking. Lon reached out and snatched it up. He began to gently blow the smouldering wood. The burned edges began to glow, to turn red as Lon coaxed the ember into life again. He reached out with his left hand and picked up one of the fused sticks of dynamite, gently touching the end of the fuse to the glowing wood. The fuse sputtered into life, seemed to fail, then sparked fiercely, the fuse burning much faster than Lon had anticipated. He lobbed the stick out across the compound, into the drifting cloud of smoke and dust. It went off with a sickening crunch. Lon heard men yell. One began to scream. Lon began to toss burning dynamite sticks out through the door at regular intervals, criss-crossing the compound.

He saved the last stick. This one he lit, placed on top of the other boxes of dynamite, and then snatched up his rifle and got out of the storeroom fast. Outside the door he turned to the left, following the stone wall across one side of the compound. There was still enough dust and powdersmoke around to conceal him and he reached the far side of the compound without being challenged. There was an arched opening in front of him. Lon slipped through and found himself in a walled garden, and in that instant the whole world seemed to explode around him in smoke and flame and noise. The ground rocked beneath his feet. Adobe walls cracked. Windows shattered. Men yelled. Horses screamed in pure terror. The stone arch Lon had stepped through tilted forwards and collapsed, showering him with debris. Lon staggered away from the wall, spitting dust from his mouth. A mixture of debris rained down out of the smoke-darkened sky. It pattered to earth all around him, some hitting him.

Crouching low Lon ran across a lush lawn. He could see a door on the far side of the garden that appeared to lead into the main house. The door opened at his touch, revealing a long, tiled passage. He ran to the far end — and found himself in a large, airy room. At the far end was a huge open fireplace with a carved stone surround. Heavy wooden furniture filled the room and the floor was littered with thick carpets and rugs. Paintings and weapons adorned the panelled walls.

Lon closed the door behind him, sliding home the metal bolt so that no one would be able to follow him through from that direction. He moved across the big room, not certain of his next move. All he could do, he realised, was to play the way the game was dealt — to make his moves as and when the situation demanded.

He was halfway across the room

when he heard a commotion coming from the other side of the double doors on the far side of the room. There was a sudden crash of sound. A man yelled. Shots rang out, and then the double doors crashed wide open . . .

14

THE winding streets of Pueblo Diablo led them ever closer to the big hacienda. Riding the horses that had belonged to Butler and Radigan, Bodie and Victoria made their way to the big house without interference. The town was pretty well deserted. Its occupants were staying indoors — a damn wise move, Bodie figured.

Victoria led the way up to the hacienda. The high gates were open. Bodie distrusted the initial impression of stately calm.

He was right to. Gunfire shattered the calm. It came from somewhere behind the hacienda. There was a slight pause and them more shots came. Men began to shout.

"Welcome home," Bodie said.

Victoria glanced at him. "Could it

be your friend? Lon?"

They rode towards the front of the house. As they neared it a sudden explosion shattered windows and sent a plume of smoke high into the air.

Bodie swung down out of the saddle, snatching his Colt from its holster. He wasn't sure what was happening, but whatever it was it seemed likely to upset the routine of the place, which could only be good for him.

The hacienda's front doors opened and two men came out. They caught sight of Victoria and moved towards her. One of them glanced at Bodie. Almost instantly his expression changed and he went for his gun, yelling, "Hey — you ain't one of . . . !"

It was as far as he got before Bodie shot him, driving two bullets through the man's chest. The gunman twisted off balance and went down without a sound, his blood splashing the pale stone steps. The second gunman moved fast, turning and diving over the low wall edging the steps. He

186

landed in the thick shrubbery fronting the house, vanished for a few seconds and came up firing. Bodie, though, had anticipated the move, and in the short time the gunman was out of sight, the manhunter ran up the steps, turned, and had a clear shot when the man raised himself up from the shrubbery. The gunman realised his slip and jerked himself round in a desperate attempt to outshoot Bodie. He was far too late. Bodie picked him off with ease, his shots ripping bloody holes through the gunman's throat and head, tossing him back against the wall of the house.

As Victoria joined Bodie a series of explosions rocked the big house. They slipped in through the big doors. Bodie pushed Victoria to one side as they moved across the wide entrance hall.

They were in the centre of the hall when the biggest explosion of all ripped through the house. The floor rippled under their feet; oil paintings fell from the walls; the sound of breaking glass echoed through the building; a jagged crack appeared in a wall on the far side of the hall and plaster dust drifted down from the ceiling.

"You any idea where your father might be?" Bodie asked.

"Si." Victoria said. She pointed across the hall. "Through there we can reach his study. It is where he spends much of his time."

"Let's give it a try," Bodie said.

Boots clattered on the tiled floor. Bodie spun round as a burly Mexican, a revolver in each hand, dashed across the hall. Bodie shoved Victoria aside as he saw the Mexican raise the guns. Bodie lunged forward, diving low, tilting the muzzle of the Colt up just before he triggered a single shot.

The bullet took the big Mexican over the heart, splintering a rib before it ploughed on into the pumping organ. His fingers jerked back on the triggers of his guns, the shots blasting into the tiled floor. Spitting blood the Mexican crashed to the floor, and his great bulk slithered loosely across the slippery tiles.

Bodie stood up, thumbing empty casings from his Colt and reloading. Then he turned to where Victoria sat huddled up against the wall, her face buried in her hands.

"Come on," he said, his tone almost gentle.

He walked ahead of her to the double doors of the room she had indicated, put his shoulder to them and smashed them wide open, and came face to face with Lon Walker!

"That you makin' all that din?" Bodie asked.

Lon nodded. "From what I just heard you ain't exactly tiptoed your way in!"

"You making for anywhere in particular?" Bodie inquired.

Lon waved a finger in the direction of the door at the far end of the big room. "Was figuring on tryin' that direction."

Bodie grinned. "So were we," he said.

"Go ahead," Lon said as they reached the door.

Bodie put out a hand and turned the handle, shoved the door open, and they all stepped inside.

Bodie had a quick impression of a large room, the walls covered by book-filled shelves. A stone fireplace dominated one end wall. High windows looked out across the rear of the hacienda, the area now a dust-fogged, devastated ruin in the wake of Lon's explosions. A tall cabinet held an assortment of rifles and handguns. Facing the door was a huge desk and behind it sat the man Bodie had seen leading the gathered riders away from the hacienda during the false attack on the mine: Don Armando Castillo.

"Victoria!"

Bodie heard the doors slam shut behind Lon. He sensed Victoria moving to his side. She made no response to her father's greeting. He did not speak to her again, but turned his attention to Bodie.

"So you are the one who has caused me so much trouble!" Castillo said. "I hoped that we would meet eventually — before you died!"

"You sure it's going to be that way?" Bodie asked.

"If he ain't, sinner, then I am!"

The words came from the direction of a high-backed leather armchair that stood in front of the fireplace. A figure leaned out from behind the high back, and the hand held a cocked gun. The pale, gaunt face and wild eyes could only have belonged to the man named Preacher Kane.

"Move one inch, manhunter, and I'll blow the lady's head right off her shoulders!" Kane said as he stood up. "You hear me too, Indian!".

"If you figure to do it, Kane, you'd better get on with it — because if you don't I aim to go right on and cause a hell of a lot more trouble!"

"For me?" Castillo said. "I think not,

Bodie. You are not on American soil now. This is Mexico and here the rules are different. You will die and no one will ever be the wiser."

"I will know, Father," Victoria said. "Or are you planning to have me killed too?"

"Child!" Castillo snapped. "When I have resolved this matter you will once again take your place in this household under my direction! There will be no talk of threats, Victoria, because you have no strength behind your words. I have too much at stake to worry over the lives of two Americans or the juvenile rantings of a hysterical woman!"

"And what about the people you took from my village?" Lon asked.

Castillo sighed. "Those peasants? I fail to understand why you worry over them. People of no consequence. If you understood the ways of Mexico you would not waste your time on such trivial matters . . . "

A wild roar burst from Lon's

throat, his anger overriding his caution. Ignoring the gun that Preacher Kane held on him, the Kiowa lunged forward.

"Lon — no!" Bodie warned.

Kane's gun went off with a thunderous crash. The bullet caught Lon in the chest. It failed to halt the Kiowa's charge. He slammed into the Comanchero, and the two of them, locked together, reeled across the room.

Bodie, realising that Castillo would not be standing idly by, took a long step towards the desk. He caught a glimpse of the Grandee straightening up from an open drawer, a revolver in his right hand. Catching hold of the edge of the big desk Bodie lifted it, tipping it back towards Castillo. A pained shout came from the Mexican as the dead weight of the huge desk slid him back against the wall, then pinned his legs to the floor.

As Bodie pulled away from the overturned desk he felt a sudden, smashing blow strike the small of his back. He was slammed against the desk, a heavy weight pressing him down. He arched his body round, fighting against the pressure on his back. Something slid around his neck and he felt his windpipe being crushed. He realised then that it had to be Preacher Kane. The Comanchero's knees were pressuring his spine while the man's arm coiled itself round his neck. He could feel Kane's hot breath against the back of his neck.

Bodie began to choke, and there was a sudden roaring sound in his ears. Black spots swam before his eyes. He felt his Colt slide from his fingers. In desperation he brought up both hands, groping for a hold — any hold, anywhere. He had to break Kane's grip on his throat. Deep down inside him, yet growing stronger with each passing second, he could feel the first stirrings of panic, and he knew he had to free himself — soon.

His clawing fingers caught hold of something. It felt like Kane's shirt. Bodie hooked his fingers in tight. He jerked and felt Kane's body slip to one side a little. He pulled some more and Kane's knees released their pressure on his spine. Bodie dragged one knee under him, getting some leverage against the floor. He thrust upwards, away from the desk, and as he regained his feet he swung Kane's body away from him. The Comanchero, his feet clear of the floor, was unable to stop himself, and Bodie let his own body be dragged round by the momentum of the swing. When he had faced about he let his body fall back, jamming Kane against the upthrust edge of the desk. A hoarse gasp broke from Kane's lips. His grip on Bodie's throat slackened. Bodie slammed a hard elbow into Kane's exposed stomach. The man grunted in pain, slipping to the floor, throwing out his hands to stop himself, and he was on his hands and knees when Bodie turned to face him.

Bodie lashed out with the toe of his boot, smashing it into Kane's side. A rib cracked under the impact. As

Kane tried to crawl away Bodie ground the heel of his boot down onto his hand. Kane cried out in pain. He threw himself at Bodie's legs, his body twisting violently. As Bodie stepped back he caught sight of the silver-bladed knife in Kane's good hand. The blade flashed swiftly, catching the light as it arced up at Bodie's body. The keen tip sliced through the material of Bodie's pants, cleaving a long gash in the manhunter's thigh. Blood pulsed from the wound.

Kane lunged to his feet, the knife held before him. He was beginning to smile despite the pain he must have felt. He came at Bodie, stumbling slightly, his left hand dangling at his side, dripping blood onto the floor.

Bodie pulled his body away from the searching tip of the blade. He reached for his own knife and found the sheath empty; the weapon must have slipped from its sheath during his initial struggle with Kane. A soft laugh rose in Kane's throat as he realised that Bodie had no weapon. He closed in quickly now, the top of the knife tearing open the front of Bodie's shirt. Another pass and the blade barely missed Bodie's throat. Bodie jerked hurriedly away, half turning, and smashed heavily into the glass-fronted gun cabinet that stood against the wall at his back. Glass showered him, a sliver gashing his face just above one eye. Bodie ignored the broken glass tearing his flesh as he pressed back against the cabinet, and used it as a solid base from which to thrust himself at Kane. He ducked beneath the Comanchero's knife, slamming his left shoulder into Kane's stomach. Kane staggered back, clutching his injured body. Bodie followed him, slapping aside the hand clutching the knife, and slamming blow after blow to the gaunt face. Kane staggered back across the room, his body twitching each time Bodie hit him. Blood sprayed from his battered face. He lost his footing and fell back against the wall. Through the blood that streaked his face he glared at Bodie with his wild eyes. He suddenly became aware of the knife in his hand. It glittered in a deadly half-circle. Bodie caught hold of Kane's wrist, twisting it brutally. Kane tried to wriggle out of his grasp. The two slid along the wall, their weight pressing against the nearest of the room's windows. The thin glass cracked and shattered. Bodie shoved hard and Kane's body bent back over the window frame. Twisting the hand which held the knife, Bodie put all his weight on it and drove the blade deep into Kane's taut throat. Kane screamed, the sound rapidly changing to a muted gurgle. Blood erupted from his mouth. Bodie stepped away from him, leaving the Comanchero hanging across the sill, his legs kicking helplessly as he died, slowly and painfully.

Bodie took a hesitant step away from the window, wiping blood from his face. He began to turn, then stopped as he heard the familiar click of a gun being cocked.

He cursed himself for every kind of a fool. He'd forgotten about Armando Castillo. But the Grandee hadn't forgotten about him!

Bodie twisted his body aside in a desperate move to get out of range of the gun. He heard the crash of the shot and the bullet smashed into the wall inches from his head. Plaster exploded away from the hole.

Facing about Bodie caught a glimpse of Castillo. Somehow he'd freed his legs from beneath the desk and had found his gun. Braced against the top edge of the desk he was cocking the gun for a second time when a gun blasted from across the room. A second shot followed. Castillo grunted. He flew back from the desk, driven against the wall by the heavy bullets. The front of his white shirt turned red. Castillo's gun went off, his bullet ploughing into the ceiling. His head thudded back against the wall, mouth dropping open, blood frothing from it. For a moment his gaze held Bodie's, the eyes still blazing, angry, defiant, then glazing with pain and death.

Bodie turned and saw Lon Walker half-sitting against the wall. The Kiowa's chest was a pulsing mass of blood. He held a smoking gun in one hand.

"You took your time over that shot," Bodie said as he knelt beside the Indian.

Lon smiled. "I didn't want to hit the wrong son of a bitch," he said, and passed out.

"I will fetch help," Victoria said.

She went to the door and opened it. A bunch of white-clad servants were gathered in the room beyond. They stared over Victoria's shoulder with curious eyes.

"Maria," Victoria said.

A fat, middle-aged woman pushed to the front of the group. "Si, Senorita Castillo!"

"Go and bring Pascal. I have instructions for him. Then I wish to see Garcia and Julio. I also want someone to go to the cabin of Tomas

Silvana, and bring him back to the hacienda. He must be well looked after. I will hold you responsible, Maria. Do you understand?"

"Si, senorita. But what will Don Castillo say? He does not favour Tomas Silvana."

Victoria's voice abruptly held an edge of steel. "Don Castillo is dead!" she said evenly, and ignoring the collective gasp she added, "He is no longer patron of this house. From now on you will all take instructions from me. I am now mistress of Hacienda Castillo!"

Bodie couldn't help but glance at her. He saw the way she held herself. Noticed the new authority in her voice. He smiled.

'*I am now mistress of Hacienda Castillo!*'

That was what she'd said. And by God so she damn well was!

15

THE death of Don Armando Castillo had far-reaching effects on everyone concerned with the great estate.

Victoria assumed control of the affairs with an ease that was sometimes frightening to watch. Bodie, who stayed close by her side during the next week found he was constantly being surprised at her knowledge of the way things were run. He quickly realised that the estate would in no way suffer from the loss of Don Castillo. From what he could see it was more likely to benefit.

One of the first things that Victoria did was to close down the silver mine and free Lon's people. The Kiowas were brought back to the hacienda, fed and clothed, and their wounds tended to. The hacienda's big kitchen was preparing food without pause.

Lon Walker was pulled through by the diligence of Victoria's nursing. After the bullet had been dug out of his chest he was settled in one of the upstairs rooms. The constant care he received made it impossible for him to do anything but get well.

Other matters were not so easily dealt with. There were still a number of Preacher Kane's Comancheros around. They were reluctant to quit the hacienda and the promise of good money. It took the combined forces of the Castillo vaqueros and Bodie's ready gun to finally convince them. There was a short, sharp gunfight. Two Comancheros died, another took a bullet in the leg, and the rest figured it wasn't worth the trouble.

The Mexican pistoleros who had hired on to aid Don Castillo rode out the minute they realised that the Don was dead.

One of the jobs Bodie undertook was to ride up to the canyon in the hills and look for Father Lucero. He was certain that the priest was dead. To his surprise, and relief, he found that the priest was alive and well. Father Lucero explained that he had almost come under the guns of the raiding Mexicans and Americans, but had foregone his dignity in a desperate attempt to escape from them: he had waited for an opportune moment and had then run, finding cover in the dense timber behind the cabin. He had stayed hidden until the canyon became deserted, and had eventually returned to the cabin to rest and recover from the beating he'd received. Father Lucero returned to the hacienda with Bodie and stayed to help Victoria.

★ ★ ★

"You sure you got to go, Bodie?" Lon asked. He was propped up in a cane armchair, watching the manhunter prepare his horse.

"Nothing to keep me here any longer," Bodie said. In a way that wasn't strictly true, because Victoria had asked him to stay; in fact she'd been asking every night, using her pliant, sensual body to great effect. But the signs were clear as far as Bodie was concerned. Life at the hacienda was fine. It was slow, measured, leisurely. There was plenty to eat, plenty to drink. The weather was fine and the evenings were full of surprises.

That was the problem: it was becoming too predictable, too comfortable. And Bodie couldn't stand the stifling effect it was having on him. He had business to conduct. There was the problem of collecting his bounty money on Preacher Kane's Comancheros. Kane himself had been buried, along with all the dead resulting from Lon's explosive episode, so Bodie wasn't going to have tangible proof that the bunch had been broken up. He figured he'd have to do it through his ex-boss Lannigan. Bodie couldn't see any problem there. Bodie had done Lannigan a favour by getting rid of the crooked law in Petrie. So the man owed him! Lannigan wouldn't like getting involved, but he wouldn't have much choice. And Bodie figured he was entitled to as much bounty as he could get from this job. He'd gone through enough to collect it. And anyhow, the money never lasted him long. A couple of weeks living it up soon cut down a fat roll of bills. If he took the flyer through to San Francisco it would be gone in less time. A man could have himself one hell of a time in Frisco, but he paid for every damn minute of it.

"You going back with your people?" Bodie asked the Kiowa.

Lon shrugged. "Maybe I'll ride 'em back to the village. See they get settled again."

"You ain't staying with 'em?"

"No." Lon glanced up at Bodie. "I can't go back to that now, Bodie," he said. "I ain't no damn reservation Indian. Hell, Bodie, could you?"

"Ain't no such thing as going back,

I suppose. You move on and life changes. It changes you and it changes whatever you left behind. You go back it just ain't what you left."

"Plenty of cattle outfits I can choose from. I'll find my way. And someday I'll find whatever it is I'm looking for."

Bodie took the Kiowa's hand. "Maybe see you sometime, Lon," he said. "You take care now, you crazy Indian!"

"Yeah, sure," Lon said. "You too, Bodie."

★ ★ ★

Victoria was waiting at the front of the hacienda.

"I do not want you to go, Bodie," she said.

"Ain't that far I can't ride down to see you one day," he said.

Victoria pouted for a second. "I am very selfish," she admitted. "I want you for myself, Bodie. I do not like to think of any other women sharing you."

"Honey, you make it sound like I was a plucked chicken straight out of the oven."

"A chicken you are not," Victoria smiled. She put her arms round him. "Can I not persuade you to stay longer?"

"I've stayed long enough, Victoria. Best I go now — before it gets too complicated."

"I should know there is no way to hold a breeze in my hand," she said wistfully. "You are like the breeze, Bodie. You come out of nowhere and linger for a while. And you bring fresh scents, strange feelings — and then you go."

Bodie climbed into the saddle. "One day I'll come calling," he promised. "When you've had time to make something of this place."

"I hold you to that. And I will make something. The Castillo name will be as it was before. A good name, Bodie. A fine, proud name."

Bodie raised his hand and touched

his heels to his horse, taking it across the terrace and out through the high gates of the Hacienda Castillo. Once clear of the town he turned the animal to the north and rode on . . .

THE END

TOP HAND
Wade Everett

The Broken T was big. But no ranch is big enough to let a man hide from himself.

GUN WOLVES OF LOBO BASIN
Lee Floren

The Feud was a blood debt. When Smoke Talbot found the outlaws who gunned down his folks he aimed to nail their hide to the barn door.

SHOTGUN SHARKEY
Marshall Grover

The westbound coach carrying the indomitable Larry and Stretch headed for a shooting showdown.

FIGHTING RAMROD
Charles N. Heckelmann

Most men would have cut their losses, but Frazer counted the bullets in his guns and said he'd soak the range in blood before he'd give up another inch of what was his.

LONE GUN
Eric Allen

Smoke Blackbird had been away too long. The Lequires had seized the Blackbird farm, forcing the Indians and settlers off, and no one seemed willing to fight! He had to fight alone.

THE THIRD RIDER
Barry Cord

Mel Rawlins wasn't going to let anything stand in his way. His father was murdered, his two brothers gone. Now Mel rode for vengeance.

ARIZONA DRIFTERS
W. C. Tuttle

When drifting Dutton and Lonnie Steelman decide to become partners they find that they have a common enemy in the formidable Thurston brothers.

TOMBSTONE
Matt Braun

Wells Fargo paid Luke Starbuck to outgun the silver-thieving stagecoach gang at Tombstone. Before long Luke can see the only thing bearing fruit in this eldorado will be the gallows tree.

HIGH BORDER RIDERS
Lee Floren

Buckshot McKee and Tortilla Joe cut the trail of a border tough who was running Mexican beef into Texas. They stopped the smuggler in his tracks.

BRETT RANDALL, GAMBLER
E. B. Mann

Larry Day had the choice of running away from the law or of assuming a dead man's place. No matter what he decided he was bound to end up dead.

THE GUNSHARP
William R. Cox

The Eggerleys weren't very smart. They trained their sights on Will Carney and Arizona's biggest blood bath began.

THE DEPUTY OF SAN RIANO
Lawrence A. Keating and
Al. P. Nelson

When a man fell dead from his horse, Ed Grant was spotted riding away from the scene. The deputy sheriff rode out after him and came up against everything from gunfire to dynamite.

FARGO: MASSACRE RIVER
John Benteen

The ambushers up ahead had now blocked the road. Fargo's convoy was a jumble, a perfect target for the insurgents' weapons!

SUNDANCE: DEATH IN THE LAVA
John Benteen

The Modoc's captured the wagon train and its cargo of gold. But now the halfbreed they called Sundance was going after it . . .

HARSH RECKONING
Phil Ketchum

Five years of keeping himself alive in a brutal prison had made Brand tough and careless about who he gunned down . . .